Where the Condor Flies

By the same author

The Land Grabbers
The Man From Socorro
Warbuck
Oliver's Kingdom

Where the Condor Flies

CURT LONGBOW

A Black Horse Western

ROBERT HALE · LONDON

ISBN 0 7090 6797 6

Robert Hale Limited
Clerkenwell House
Clerkenwell Green
London EC1R 0HT

BBRA		BCRO	
BASH		BGRE	
BBIN		BHAR	
BBIR		BSAN	
BCON		BWHI	02/01

Typeset by
Derek Doyle & Associates, Liverpool
Printed and bound in Great Britain by
Antony Rowe Limited, Wiltshire

Prologue

The boom of the guns went on unceasingly. Screams of wounded men merged with the yells of Santa Anna's hand-picked seasoned fighting men. A pall of smoke hung over what had been the fortified mission known locally as the Alamo. General Santa Anna himself watched the disintegration of the massive walls, punctured by cannonballs. He smiled at Coronel Fernandez, who, sweated and bloody leaned gasping on his sword.

'You did well, Luis, to breach the southern gate. Soon it will be all over!'

Coronel Fernandez wiped a mixture of sweat and gunpowder from his eyes,squinted at him.

'And then what? Do we take prisoners?'

The general frowned and pursed his lips.

'There are women and children in the enclosure. We give them clear passage. The Texans...' he shook his head. 'We have no use for rebel Texans. Give the order. No prisoners!'

Coronel Fernandez grinned, his handsome Mexican features twisted into a diabolical gargoyle mask. General Santa Anna looked at him with distaste. It was one thing to give an order of execution but another to enjoy the outcome.

Fernandez saluted.

'As you order, General!'

'Then see to it . . . and *Coronel* . . .'

'*Sí, General?*'

'God go with you, *Coronel*, and don't enjoy your orders too much. The good God will be watching!'

The *coronel* saluted smartly, turned on his heel and left the small tent, thinking the *general* was a lucky swine. He gave the orders and kept his hands clean. Who was he to judge if a man enjoyed killing? That was why men joined the army, to fight and kill.

He rejoined his unit and gave orders to his bugler to sound the regrouping battle-charge. They were now ready to breach the crumbling walls and overrun the remaining defenders who'd stood out against the onlsaught for twelve days. Surely today would see the end of the siege of the Alamo.

Before the bugler drew breath, another trumpet sounded. It came from within the walls. Someone inside was giving the last rallying call. It was an unearthly sound. Unnerving, like the wailing of the dead who wouldn't lie down.

It caused superstitious shivers to run up and down the tired Mexican soldiers as they gathered the last of their strength and courage for the last magnificent charge.

'Sound the charge, damn you!' shouted Coronel Fernandez, knowing full well that tired troops could easily lose their courage as death or glory stared them in the face.

The bugler responded, the clear notes cutting through the smoke and gunpowder fumes; then the last wave of deperate men began to cut down the defending Texans, who were already weakened by lack of water and starvation rations.

The trumpet played on as the massacre began. Fires raged and over all could be heard the screams and cries of women and children cowering in what had been the great hall of the mission.

Soon it was over. The trumpet ceased and General Santa Anna was aware of a sense of relief tempering the heady triumph.

There was a stench of blood and human excrement pervading the air polluted with the smoke from fires and gunpowder fumes. The triumphant Mexicans moved in waves as they breached the walls and annihilated the few pitiful defenders.

Soon the compound was silent and all quiet as the men sought out those who might be hiding but, apart from the fearful bunch of women and children, the defenders were dead.

The *coronel* reported to the *general*.

'It is done, Excellency, as you ordered. Only the women and children left alive.'

'Good. See that they are fed and taken to San Antonio. Tonight, the men can celebrate. Tomorrow, we shall ransack the Alamo and burn it to the ground. We shall leave nothing but the ruins as a lesson for the rebels for all time!'

Ben Jackson, the bugler, sixteen years old, lay shivering in the cesspit. He clutched his once-shiny brass trumpet close to his breast. Now, he and it were covered in human slime as his father, Sergeant Jackson, had commanded when he had realized all was lost. He had come, bloody and staggering with weakness to find Ben, who had been courageously playing his trumpet as an encouragement to the few remaining Texans.

Ben had ceased abruptly when he saw his father's ghastly face and knew that this would be the last time he would see his father alive.

'Go, son. You are too young to die! Hide yourself in the cesspit. Better a mouthful of shit than to die under the hands of the Mexicans. Remember me always, boy. I love you and am proud of you and I want you to live. Someday you may revenge yourself on that cold murdering bastard, Coronel Fernandez, known as General Santa Anna's executioner. Your age wouldn't save you!'

There had been a quick hug and Sergeant Jackson had disappeared into the fog of battle. Young Ben, hesitating a moment, torn between love for his father and fear, made his mind up. Scrambling and running doubled up, he made for the stable block where lay the great cesspit. Dragging the grating aside, he took a deep breath and plunged down into the stinking bubbling mass. He clung on to the rung of the rusted ladder used for maintenance work, nearly fainting at the stench.

He could hear the muffled roar of cannon and the screams of dying men. He shivered and vomited and didn't stir when later the grating was lifted for a moment as someone took a cursory glance.

'Nothing down there but a load of shit,' a Mexican voice murmured and the grating clanged down.

Ben Jackson never knew how long he stayed there, but it was nearly dawn when he found the courage to climb out and collapse on the stable floor. All was quiet.

Then staggering outside to breathe in fresh air, he smelled the sweet rotten stench of death; already the buzzards were flapping their wings and alighting to pluck at the flesh of the rotting bodies. . . .

Years later, Ben Jackson still awakened from nightmares sweating and shaking; the hate for Santa Anna and Luis Fernandez was as strong and bitter in his mouth then as it had been as a boy.

He became a loner. He lived high in the mountains and when the nightmares rode him he played his trumpet and the *campesinos* in the valleys heard and shook their heads.

'The mad Texan lives the siege of the Alamo all over again.'

9

But all that was going to change. Jeff Onslow was a stranger to the mountains. He was a marshal with a mission. He was looking for the man known as El Condor. A man most savage. A pitiless man who wasn't content with robbing trains but massacred everyone on board whether they were railroad men, passengers, or women and children.

He had gathered to himself a bunch of wild men, recruited from the Mexican army and now, thirty years after the siege of the Alamo, held the country in thrall.

His name was whispered if at all. It was said he had informers in every *taverna*. That he paid well for information. No one could identify El Condor. He lived high in the mountains, in an eyrie which was a fortress in itself.

His temper was short and his power far-reaching.

Jeff Onslow was facing the toughest task of his career.

One

The nightmares were all around him, cannons booming, screams and the pitiless shrieks of shells exploding somewhere behind him. It was raining. He could hear, behind all the noise and confusion, the heavy drip of water cascading over the rocks outside his bolthole. He gripped the trumpet tightly and played on, to drown out the noise and spur on the ghostly comrades fighting all around him.

Outside the rocky cave the dark pall of night lifted, and with it the thunderstorm gradually died away as a new day dawned. Far down below in Horse Creek Valley the *campesinos* went about their business as usual.

'Did you hear the crazy one playing his trumpet?' an old man asked his neighbour as he herded his flock of sheep along the road to the open pasture.

'*Sí.* The idiot fool kept my *bambino* awake and Juanita is bad-tempered and thinks we should band

11

together and run him out of the hills.'

'How can we do that? He is harmless. Why, the children run after him when he comes into the village. He gives them sugar and hazelnuts and tells them stories about Santa Anna and how the Texicans fought so hard before they died at the siege of the Alamo!'

'All the same, he is getting worse. If it wasn't for El Condor . . .'

'Hush! Don't speak his name.' The old man looked around as if someone might overhear their conversation. 'You know he has spies everywhere.'

'All the same, if it wasn't for him, we should have ridden out and found the trumpet man and got rid of him.'

'If you-know-who can't find him, how could we? You're talking out of the back of your neck, Luis.'

Luis grunted and watched the old man move his sheep along. It was all right for him. He didn't have a wife who grumbled or a wailing infant to deal with. Luis went back to his blacksmith's shop, suppressing a yawn. He was looking forward to siesta-time and it couldn't come soon enough.

Far above the valley the range of hills reared and dipped. Ben Jackson had found a secluded place where over the years he'd built himself a cosy homestead. It was in a small bowl of land at the bottom of which was a tiny spring, a trickle of water which found its way down from somewhere higher up. It spouted forth amongst some rocks and around it had grown a small oasis of greenery. Surrounding it were the sparse windblown rocks of the high sierras.

Gradually he had scooped out a cave and carried the rocks to make a strong hidden home, the inside of which had been smoothed with clay from around the spring itself. In front of it he had built a stone wall as a windbreak. It also hid the cave from any casual passer-by, if indeed anyone should find this verdant hollow; up to now no one had.

As the years passed he'd fashioned a rough-and-ready fireplace at the far end of the cave and constructed a crude chimney of stone. When the wind was in the wrong direction it caused a draught which burned up his logs too quickly, but that was a small price to pay for the warmth of the fire and the means to cook his meat in an old soot-blackened iron pot which hung on a tripod, and when the glowing embers were just right, he could cook his cornmeal pan-bread on an old frying-pan. It was all he needed. He had a cosy home, with animal skins laid over a mound of hay, gathered each summer, for a bed.

Sometimes Ben Jackson thought back to the days of his childhood when both parents were alive and he played with other soldiers' children. It was then that he missed the company of others. But the memories also brought pain and anger as he thought of his father's death at the Alamo, and the man he'd watched carrying out with such enjoyment General Santa Anna's orders to kill all survivors. He would never forget that man's face. It haunted him when the nightmares closed in on him. . . .

El Condor, grey-haired with a sweeping moustache that covered most of his lower face and jaw, raised his wide-brimmed sombrero and waved it above his head at the bunch of Comancheros hiding in the nooks and crannies of the rearing cliffs on each side of the railway track. It was the signal that the train, long overdue, was coming.

In the distance they heard the *whoo hoo* of the whistle as it chugged around the last bend before reaching the gradient as the railway entered the foothills and went into the tunnel that cut through the mountains. The engine slowed to a crawl as it puffed its way upwards, belching black smoke as the fireman sweated to feed the furnace.

As it came around the last corner El Condor waved again. This time the look-out man slashed the ropes holding a stout tree-trunk upright. It fell with a resounding thwack right across the railway line, shattering and displacing the rails.

The train chugged on but then came the scream of brakes as the engine ploughed into tree and branches and finally came to a stop, half on and half off the rails at a drunken angle.

There were the screams of frightened male and female passengers, and shouts from angry rail officials, and then utter silence as El Condor's Comancheros swooped down from their hiding-places, firing their rifles and yelling like demons.

Then the doors were wrenched open and evil, smiling Mexicans swarmed in. The shocked passengers were herded like cattle off the train and lined up shivering, the men cowering and voluntarily bringing out wallets and watches and the womenfolk trying to hide their jewellery down lowcut cleavages in the earnest belief that no gentleman would violate their person.

It was a mistake. El Condor himself claimed the privilege of tearing off the bodices of old and young women alike and retrieving their pitiful pieces of jewellery and other treasured gewgaws.

One woman spat in his face, her dark eyes flashing. She stood proud with bare bosom exposed. It was as if she flaunted herself deliberately.

'Bastard! Eater of dog shit! May you rot in hell and may your balls drop off!'

He silenced her with an open-handed slap across her face, which felled her to the ground.

'Silence, woman! Don't you realize it's dangerous to anger El Condor?'

'What does it matter? You will kill us all anyway!' She spat at him again as she lay on the ground.

He watched her. She reminded him of a cat cornered, defeated but not tamed.

'Who are you? What is your name?'

'My name is none of your business! Kill me and have done!'

He bent down and grabbed her wrist and hauled

her upright, then twisted her arm up her back. He could smell her perfume and her sweat and it moved him. This was a woman who bathed and looked after her body. She was not in her first youth, but young enough to have a ripe and firm body.

Against his rule about such things, he was interested in her as a woman. He glanced at Julio, his second-in-command.

'Take her and don't let her go, while I do what has to be done.' He thrust her into Julio's arms and strode away to walk down the rest of the line of fearful passengers. Then he inspected the pile of assorted bags that lay in a heap. Already the wallets and loose money was being tossed carelessly into a stout canvas bag.

Several Comancheros waited expectantly. He nodded and turned away, ignoring the sudden staccato rattle of rifle fire and the screams of the dying.

Lucia da Silva watched with horror; if it hadn't been for Julio's tight grip on her she would have dropped to the ground. As it was, her faint was long and deep. She was on horseback when she came to and leaning against the chest of the man known as El Condor.

'What are you going to do with me?' she managed to utter.

El Condor's answer was a low growl.

'Relax, woman. You will know soon enough!'

16

TWO

Jeff Onslow was a tough ex-army sergeant, lucky to be alive after the rout in North Carolina. He'd followed General Joseph Johnston all through the general's campaigns and apart from a bullet wound in his upper left arm and recurring bouts of dysentery and fever, he considered himself one of the lucky ones.

But his homecoming had been tragic. The Yankees had burned his parents' homestead and both were dead. His fiancée had married a get-rich-quick gunrunner and gone God knows where and for a long while Jeff Onslow had become a drunken drifter.

Then one morning he'd woken up in jail in San Antonio, Mexico, with a headache which threatened to split his skull wide open. He'd crossed the Rio Grande and wandered about and had been impressed by the Mexican Dons' way of life. He admired their responsibility and their way of treating their peons as family. Even the poorest peasant

17

would share his last crust with a stranger.

Vaguely he remembered getting into a scrap because of a giant of a bully slapping a young girl because she wasn't serving him fast enough while all the other drinkers sat back and watched. He thought this most unusual, seeing they were such a cheerful laughing people.

It was only later, while he sat with head down in his cell that a fellow prisoner explained the reason why no one interfered.

'You made a mistake, my friend,' the other man grinned as if it amused him that the Americano might be in deep trouble. 'Alonzo Pescuario is rumoured to be one of El Condor's trusted lieutenants, not that anyone can prove it. But the bastard comes into town, throws his weight about and he's never short of *dinero*.' His fingers snapped together as if fingering a wad of bills.

Jeff looked at him a bit foggily, not understanding.

'And who the hell's El Condor? And what stops the mayor of this place and his men from running this Pescuario out of town for good?'

The man sat up and stared at Jeff.

'You *are* a stranger in these parts or you would have heard of El Condor and how he looks after his own. There are more than Pescuario who come into town and shoot it up! *Sí, señor!* When it gets back to El Condor that a man in San Antonio beat up Pescuario, then he and his men will come and shoot the place up and the mayor will have to tax the townsfolk to find the money to pay for the insult! You, my friend, might well finish up on the hanging tree because of the fury of the people. How you like that, eh?'

'You must be joking!'

'No, *señor*. It has happened before!'

'Hell's bells! I was helping one of your own women! Doesn't that count?'

'No, *señor*. Women don't count when it is a matter of a town's very existence!'

'Then I want to see the mayor! Isn't there a sheriff in this place?'

'No, *señor*. The mayor, he runs the town. We cannot afford the luxury of a sheriff.'

'Then I want to see the mayor right now!' Jeff got up and rattled the bars of the cell even though the noise nearly tore his head apart.

'Hey! Anyone out there?'

The other prisoner grinned shrugged, settled back and closed his eyes.

'No use shouting, *señor*. He'll come when he's ready and when it's time to eat. So I advise you to sleep!'

But the prisoner had been wrong. The mayor, a small man with a big moustache, came an hour later and opened the cell door with a huge key and indicated Jeff was to come out. The other man tried to follow but the mayor shoved him roughly back.

'Not you, Carlos, just this one here. You want coffee?' turning to Jeff.

19

'You bet!'

'Then come with me. I want to talk to you.' That was how it was that Jeff found himself sheriff of San Antonio with just his keep and no salary in lieu of a prison sentence for causing an affray, breaking up several chairs and cracking a mirror in the local *taverna*.

'But why me?' Jeff had asked, astounded.

The mayor sipped coffee and stared him out.

'*Señor*, there are not many *hombres* who would take on Alonzo Pescuario, never mind beat the horse-balls out of him. There are many townsfolk ready to back a good leader but we have not a leader amongst us. You, *señor*, fit the bill. You have heard of El Condor?'

Jeff nodded. 'That feller in the cell with me mentioned him. Bully-boy works for him, I gather.'

'We don't know for sure but as he's got money to throw around we believe so. No one has seen El Condor but wherever he and his men target, he leaves a crude calling-card with a rough sketch of a condor in flight.'

'How d'you mean, target?'

The mayor laughed. 'They're outlaws, *señor*. Comancheros. They sell guns to the Indians, and terrorize the *campesinos* in the villages. There are many tales about them. Of killings and kidnappings. El Condor has been ravaging our countryside for thirty years. Sometimes we do not hear of him for long periods. We think he crosses the Rio Grande and roams Texas and beyond. We also believe that he

20

comes back to Mexico to go into hiding when the Texans get too close to him. There have been rumours, *señor.*'

'And what do you think I can do?'

The mayor shrugged. 'We think maybe you are a military man? Maybe a Confederate soldier? You have the bearing of such a one. Not that I want to pry . . .'

Jeff smiled. 'No secret. I was a sergeant but now I'm rootless.'

'Then perhaps you would consider starting a new life here?'

Jeff grinned, then held out his hand. The mayor clasped it.

'What about the prisoner in the cell?'

'Carlos? Oh, a drunken layabout. Always in and out of jail. Mind you, he did grab the girl from under Pescuario's nose and tripped the bastard up so you could get at him.'

'Did he now? Then maybe you should free him for his services and maybe I could give him a job?'

The mayor frowned, picked his nose, and then nodded.

'Maybe you could keep him off the streets. Kick his arse now and again. At least he could show you around San Antonio.

Jeff enjoyed his new status and Carlos, though still addicted to the bottle, proved useful. After Jeff dowsed him a couple of times in the horse-trough outside the small adobe building that passed for the jail and the sheriff's office, Carlos's respect for Jeff grew and they worked well together.

San Antonio had its share of drunks and layabouts and petty thieves but none that the two men couldn't handle. Everything went smoothly, even on Saturday nights when the *campesinos* came into town to spend their wages and to repent in church the following day.

But the atmosphere in town changed when El Condor's men rode in after one of their raids across the river. They were celebrating yet another hold-up and this time an American army payroll was involved. Celebrating, the men went wild, shooting up the town, turning out the regular customers from the town's brothels and taking over the women.

Then just before dawn broke, they were in their saddles and emptying their guns in the air before galloping out of town towards the mountains.

Jeff Onslow felt sick with humiliation. He hadn't been able to do a thing about it. He'd had to watch the mayhem with Carlos, knowing that if he showed any objection he and Carlos would have been shot out of hand.

Jeff was furious.

'How in hell can I keep law and order if I don't get any back-up from the townsfolk?' he'd raved furiously at the mayor, when the mayor had come complaining about lack of control. 'We're only two men, Goddammit!'

'You're hired to defend us from that rabble!' the mayor yelled. 'Señora Alverez and her girls are threatening to leave! What will the men of this town do without the *señora* and her girls? Those dog-turds treated them disgustingly, as if they were animals. The very idea makes me sweat!' He mopped his forehead with a dirty red handkerchief.

'Then we either swear in legal deputies or we bring in mercenaries from across the river and the town pays for them. It's your choice.'

The mayor rasped his chin and considered.

'I must convene a meeting of the townsfolk, *señor.* It will mean everyone will have to pay extra tax and some will not like it.'

Jeff shrugged. 'It's your decision, Mayor. I can fork my horse any time and move on, no sweat.'

The mayor was worried.

'We'll come up with an answer, so don't start thinking of pulling out. San Antonio's improved a lot since you took over. The women at the church sewing bee were only saying the other day how they can walk the streets without hindrance, these days. They feel safe with you patrolling the town.'

'Then press the point, Mayor and get some volunteer deputies to be ready when El Condor's men come into town again.

But though they wanted protection, and Jeff Onslow to remain in charge, there were no volunteers. All the business folk of San Antonio claimed they were not fighting men and certainly no gunmen to take on the tough outlaws.

'Then that's it,' Jeff announced when the vote was taken. 'Who's for me to bring in some outside help?'

All hands shot up.

'Right, then the mayor here will organize the monetary help. We can't expect mercenaries to risk their lives for nothing!'

Jeff and Carlos went back to the office. Jeff had thought of a plan of his own. He remembered his comrades whom he'd marched with, drunk and brawled with and fought with against the Yankees. Tough Texicans who would spit on their hands and take on El Condor and his men for a lark.

He'd show these faint-hearted Mexicans how Texicans could fight.

He waited anxiously for a reply after he sent off the telegram to his old buddy, Red Baines, hoping he was still fighting and brawling his way to eternity and not belly-up underground. Red's reply made him grin. If there was a war going on down in Mexico, Red was his man and all their buddies were coming with him to liven things up a mite. Typical Red. Life was looking up.

Jeff watched the road from the north. Day by day passed and no small cavalcade arrived. Fortunately neither did El Condor's men. But Jeff heard the trumpet player, his music echoing eerily when the wind was in the right direction. Jeff wondered about him and what was the significance of the sounds.

He'd been visiting Miranda Parker at the best

brothel in town. She was very accommodating both with her affections and her hospitality; both of them had been drinking quite a bit together.

'What's the story about the trumpeter?' Jeff enquired.

Miranda, a strapping, overblown girl with a big bosom and a liking for wide shoulder-showing blouses, smoothed his cheek. She kissed him.

'Come on, lover, why talk about trumpeters when you've got me to cuddle up to?'

He grinned down at her.

'You're a glutton for punishment, you minx.' He kissed her neck, his tongue trailing. She groaned with pleasure, closing her eyes and reached for him. He forgot about the trumpeter.

The next day he saw the hearse drawn by two black horses wearing black plumes trundling down Main Street, flanked by two riders. Jeff squinted into the sun as the little cavalcade pulled up outside the saloon. He slapped his thigh and laughed as he recognized the two riders. So Red Baines had made it and with him, Ely Johnson, the hoary old gunner.

Then he took note of the three figures on the hearse. He didn't recognize the hearse but he recognized the two male figures, though not the girl sitting beside them. Wang Chen and his son, Li Chen, grinned at him as he gave a great holler and ran down the street to greet them all.

'Howdy, pal!' called Red. 'I brought all I could muster. What's new?'

Then they were all clustered around Jeff, the two Chinese grinning and nodding while the girl stood back, waiting with head bent as Red and Ely and Jeff all spoke together. Then Jeff called for order after taking a long look at the hearse.

'So, Wang, where the hell did you get that rig?'

'Won it in a card game, boss. Very handy. Fight. Kill. Bury and get paid. All very good, boss!'

'You never change, Wang, and you, Li, you've grown some since I saw you last.'

Li nodded and grinned. 'Me good fighter. Kick box and good with gun!'

'So there'll be no washing of laundry any more?'

'No sir! We in the undertaking business now. Yes sir!'

'Come in the office, all of you. I've got a bottle and we can drink and talk.' They followed him down the street to the little jail.

When they were seated, comfortable with a drink, he told them about El Condor living up in the mountains with at least twenty men, and how the outfit swooped down on the town after a raid, shot the town up, ravaged the women and drank the place out of liquor. The townsfolk were too shitscared to do anything about it.'

'And that's what you want us to do? Go against this El Condor feller? You think us mad? Twenty against us five?' Red gave Carlos a look of contempt. Carlos was sitting quietly in a corner cleaning his nails with his knife. Jeff gave him a brief glance.

'You can count Carlos in. Drunk or sober, he can handle himself.'

'But can he shoot?'

Jeff looked doubtful. 'Can you shoot, Carlos?'

Carlos looked up and nodded and then went back to his nail-cleaning.

'I can shoot.'

'There you are then. Six of us.'

'The odds are still against us.'

'We're not going to sit here until the bastards come to us again. We go hunting them and take 'em out one at a time. Remember our raiding parties? We go in as a disciplined team.'

Red Baines grunted.

'What about the kid?' He pointed a thumb at Li Chen.

'He'll stick with his pa. Wang will do as he did before and Li will back him up. None of those bastards will suspect a couple of Chinks of spying. The Rebs made the mistake of thinking Chinks only washed clothes and El Condor will think the same. Are you two willing to scout around when we find their hideout, Wang?'

Wang nodded until his head was ready to drop off.

'We move like serpents and then fight like tigers! We make way for you to follow. Then we do burying and we make fortune and please ancestors!'

'I don't know about pleasing them, but you please us,' grunted Jeff. 'Now, we got to make plans, and we keep 'em under our hats. El Condor has many spies in town, for the bastard pays well for information.'

'How does he get his information?' Red asked sharply.

Jeff shrugged.

'I suppose someone in town knows where he hangs out. We'll have to keep watch on all comings and goings for a while and see if if we can pin-point anyone special.'

'What about a bit of wrong information,' old Ely asked. 'As I see it, someone will know already who we are, after that there public meeting. Maybe me and Carlos here should buddy up and give off some careless talk. What about it, boss?'

Jeff laughed. 'That's as good an excuse as it comes for you two to drink yourselves under the table! Just as long as you don't overdo it. I think I'll sleep on it and work out a plan of action. Where will you boys stay tonight, and what about the little lady? Where will she stay?'

Li blushed and blinked.

'She stays with me in the hearse. Honourable father will stay with you.'

Jeff grinned.

'Kids soon grow up, Wang.I think you'd all better doss down in Señora Benevido's boarding-house where I'm staying. She has vacant rooms.'

Señora Benevido was only too pleased to show them small but clean rooms and offered to cook for them. Li Chen and his girlfriend ate with them and they caught up on gossip and news of old army friends.

Then after midnight, after much ribald leg-pulling, Li Chen and Lianne left them and retired to the roomy hearse. Pulling the black curtains they settled down snugly after Li had settled the horses for the night at the nearby stable, paying the ostler to feed and water them in the morning.

Jeff and Red had a last drink together after Wang and old Ely yawned and wandered off to their beds.

'Just how d'you propose to smoke the bastards out, Jeff?'

Jeff tossed off his whiskey and shrugged.

'Ely's suggestion is the only one we got at present, Red. We might get lucky, but there's a lot of ground out there to trail. Trouble is, Red, I'm still a stranger in these parts. Apart from Carlos, I can't trust even those who want me to clean up this town.'

'Hmm, so it's up to us!'

'Yeah, old buddy, and I think we're going to have to consider this as a military campaign. How would General Johnston have gone about a situation like this?'

'Sent out the scouts in the first instance. Plot the lie of the land and decide on which front to attack.'

Jeff grinned ruefully.

'Some hopes for us! We're a bit thin on the ground to be picky and choosy. I think it will be hit-and-run and surprise attacks and on the move at all times. You remember when . . .'

He stopped as a great flash and then a boom hit the night sky and the window of Señora Benevido's

29

dining-room blew in with a shower of glass and great puffs of smoke.

'What the hell . . ?' Both men leapt to their feet and rushed to the outer door, while Señora Benevido, wrapped in a shawl appeared from her kitchen, shaken and frightened.

Outside the door it was a scene from hell. The saloon was going up in smoke. Great gouts of flame spewed forth. Next door, the blacksmith's shop was ablaze, as was the stable. There were shots and screams as men fought to get out of the saloon and to add to the bedlam, the ostler was freeing the horses as the hay in the loft burst into flames.

There were men on horseback firing their guns and as the late drinkers reeled coughing and spluttering out of the saloon, the horses reared as the riders dug in their spurs and many men went down underfoot.

But what made Jeff curse was the sudden yell of Wang, who sprang forward like a madman. In his hand was the long curved knife. He was in his underwear and old Ely was right behind him.

'My son . . . my son!' Wang was scrabbling to try and wrench open the back door of the hearse, which was a mass of flame. Ely was holding him back but Wang fought like one possessed. The wooden hearse with its thick black paint was well alight. The glass in the sides had exploded but there was no sign of either the boy or girl trying to escape.

Jeff saw Wang knock Ely to the ground as he risked burns to open up what was now a funeral pyre.

The half-drunken crowd stood back as the heat increased.

Jeff drew a deep breath and caught the wiry Wang. He used his brute strength to drag him clear, then muttering a 'forgive me' he clipped Wang under the chin and caught him as he fell to the ground. Glancing at Ely, who was struggling to his feet, he said tersely, 'See to Wang,' then turned to fight his way through the crowd. He was in time to see the rearing horsemen bunching together and starting the mad gallop out of town.

He fired a couple of shots after them, and was sure he'd hit one of them as the man seemed to lurch and then settle again in the saddle before following on behind.

'You bastards!' roared Jeff. 'We'll get you, if we have to follow you to hell itself!'

Then he turned back to help organize a chain of water carriers. But it was too little too late. All the townsfolk could do was watch the saloon and the stable and the blacksmith's shop burn down and all eyes shied away from what was left of the hearse. It was now a smouldering mass of embers and somewhere amidst the red-hot debris were the corpses of two young people.

The smoke-blackened townsfolk stood exhausted, watching the last of the smouldering embers, the air thick and choking and every now and again, sparks, caught by the wind would sizzle and fresh fires were hastily beaten out.

Eduardo Antonini, his round fat belly sagging, came staggering over to Jeff. He crossed himself.

'Mother of God! What a night! I would have died if it hadn't been for Carlos!' The saloonkeeper wiped a dirty handkerchief over his face. He smelled of smoke and scorched hair. Jeff looked closer and saw his moustache half burnt off and the skin on one cheek, red raw.

'Yes, where is Carlos? I haven't seen him all night. What's happened to him?'

'He dragged me out of the saloon and went back for Marty, his old drinking pal. When those bastards came into the saloon, he slipped out and went for his gun. Pescuario was shouting his mouth off and wanting Maria whom he'd slapped when you took him on. When Maria wouldn't come out of the kitchen, he and the rest of the bastards started shooting at the men's feet making them dance around.'

'Then what?'

'Carlos came back and took a wild shot at Pescuario and missed and then all hell broke loose. One of those dung beetles had a couple of hand-grenades and lobbed one at the bar and when he ran outside he threw another at the hearse. They went off together. I was hit by the blast just as I tried to get out of the way. I hit the ground and Carlos dragged me clear and went back for Marty.'

'Is he hurt?'

'Not a bit of it. Shook up and drunk to the eyeballs but he's got the luck of the devil!'

32

Jeff found Carlos lying out cold half under a wagon tipped on its side and minus a wheel. He shook him.

'Wake up, Carlos!'

Carlos groaned and Jeff sat him up. There was blood on Carlos's cheek.

'Wha ... what happened?' He groaned again. 'I feel like hell.' He held his head in his hands.

'Carlos, wake up. You're a goddamned hero!'

'What?'

Jeff repeated his words and Carlos listened in disbelief.

'Me? I did that? It's Eduardo's home-brew that did it! Mother of God! I'm no hero!' He groaned again and rocked himself, head in hands.

Jeff shook his head and sighed. The first time he'd got a chance to make something of himself, and he had to be lumbered with this spineless greaser as his deputy. It made a man fair want to puke. He kicked Carlos in the ribs.

'Get up you drunken bum, and act like a deputy should. Don't you understand? It's going to be all-out war! There's a couple of kids been roasted alive and God knows if any one else is missing or hurt. Pull yourself together, Carlos!' He slapped Carlos on both cheeks.

Instantly Carlos's black eyes opened and for one mad moment, Jeff read death in their bleak depths. What the hell. . . ?'

Then the look faded and Carlos was his old self.

He shook himself and then said softly,

'What are we waiting for?'

They found Ely and Red Baines holding down Wang Chen who looked to be having some kind of a fit. The scrawny Chinaman was trembling violently and his thin parchment face was screwed up in silent grief. It was eerie to watch the stoical grief and the twitching limbs.

Jeff remembered when Wang had first joined their outfit. It had been in a place called Royston Plattes. The Yankees had looted and burned it to the ground and moved on and Wang and his young son and had been found by Jeff's commander, hiding in a cellar. It was all that remained of Wang's laundry. From then on, Wang had attached himself to Captain Pearson and become his batman and Li had been his messenger boy. Then, during a very scary episode of hand-to-hand fighting, Wang had shown his skill in the peculiar art of what he called kung fu, a way of fighting that confused the enemy and resulted in more than a few broken necks. Wang had become a fully paid-up member of the Confederate Army and between campaigns given Red Baines and himself some lessons in self-defence which had proved useful.

In those days he had been a lithe, slippery eel of a man, hard to hold and pin down. Now, he was a bowed shrunken figure, all dried-up sinew. Jeff felt a great pity for him and also a sense of guilt. If he hadn't sent for help, Li would still be alive.

A great hatred, which at first been just a spark, was now fanned into flame.

'I'll get those bastards and their elusive El Condor if it's the last thing I do in this life!' He shook his fist into the air as he looked at the devastation around them.

Three

The man they called El Condor was in a towering rage. He strode up and down in front of his men, who were lined up like military troops. They were a hangdog looking lot and his fury and contempt for them was plain to be seen.

'Imbeciles!' he roared,'How many times must I tell you that you do not, I repeat, do not shit in your own backyard? How many times have I told you to steer clear of San Antonio when you go to seek excitement? There are other villages where you could drink and womanize and get rid of tension! This sacking and burning of the town will surely bring out the militia. We don't want that. It would mean leaving this part of Mexico for good. Who wants to leave their families behind?'

The men looked at each other, then, one more bold than the rest spoke for the rest of them.

'If you would allow us to bring our families here, we should be more content. You have brought a woman here. Why shouldn't we have our women?'

He was referring to the woman brought back and now held a prisoner in El Condor's hut. El Condor drew himself up to his full height and his eyes glared at the man with the courage to speak.

'The reason the men with families must leave them behind is simple. If we have to move out fast, the women and children would be an encumbrance. You are free to visit your families. If you choose to carouse with the unmarried ones amongst you, then that's your affair!'

'About your woman . . .'

'That's my affair. I am not beholden to anyone here. I give the orders and up to now each one of you has accumulated more cash and goods than he would earn in a lifetime. Anyone not satisfied can get on his horse and leave now!'

The Lorenzo brothers looked at each other, the elder giving a slight nod, then without a word they both reached for their horses and sprang aboard, while the rest of the men watched in silent surprise.

The elder, Juan, gave El Condor a sloppy salute.

'My apologies, El Condor, but my brother and I think it time to leave.' Then without a glance at their erstwhile comrades, the brothers kicked their horses in the ribs and galloped towards the gap in their mountain home.

The men waited with bated breath. If the Lorenzo brothers passed through the gap, El Condor's iron control over them all would be broken.

El Condor watched them gallop away. Then, gauging the distance, he coolly snatched up his rifle, took careful aim and snapped off two shots. The watching men saw both the brothers throw up their arms and somersault off their horses.

Julio spat on the ground, his eyes hard.

'They had it coming to them. Two of you catch the horses and you, Luc, make up a burying detail. We don't want the buzzards flying around for spying eyes to see.'

El Condor turned to go back to his hut. He saw Lucia da Silva watching out of the window. But he had far more on his mind than Lucia. His spies had reported a train on its way from Laredo with instructions to pull up at a small stop called Sanderson's Halt. From there the payroll for Fort Stockton would be transferred to a waiting military convoy to take it by road to its destination.

El Condor's agile brain had exulted at the thought of another crack at the Texicans. It should be feasible to stop the train before it reached Sanderson Halt, rob the express car and be away before the alarm was sounded. The plan needed working on, and hideouts arranged. The country would be swarming with soldiers and until they could cross the Rio Grande back into Mexico, it would be a case of cat and mouse.

Lucia da Silva watched as the man she knew as El Condor came back to the hut. She knew he had seen her and he would know that she had witnessed the murder of the two men. Not that it mattered to her about the death of the brothers. They had been just two more enemies to despise. But she was a witness to the killings. El Condor would now never allow her to leave the high mountain eyrie alive, no matter what ransom was offered to release her. He was wealthy enough not to be tempted by money.

She knew he would use her until he tired of her and she faced the realization that he would put a bullet in her without hesitation when her usefulness was over.

Lucia da Silva had never had it easy. She'd had to fight for what she wanted all her life. Born the daughter of a hardworking peon whose family had worked for generations for Don da Silva's family, she'd caught the eye of the old don when she was seventeen and he in his sixties and already the father of grown-up children. Her life had been easy for the few years the old man had left. But when he died, her life changed. The oldest son, Luis paid her a pittance and turned her out of the family hacienda. She'd been on her way to Montelova to start a new life when El Condor had held up the train.

Now she knew she would have to use her brains and her body to survive. She'd noticed the youth, barely nineteen, who seemed to do all the menial tasks in the camp. He fetched water from the tiny stream running down the mountain and emptied bucket slops as well as helping the greasy fat cook to prepare meals. She wondered if he was touched by God and not quite right in the head.

He always smiled at her when he brought her food. The most important thing was that no one watched him. He could come and go as he pleased, as if too unimportant to worry about.

She wondered if he'd ever been with a woman. . . .

Because of the high altitude of the camp and its situation in the midst of a dip in the mountains, she was allowed to wander free if she wanted to. She rarely did this, for the men's eyes followed her and if it hadn't been for fear of El Condor, those men would have fought and killed to possess her.

El Condor, in his arrogance and cruelty, had forewarned her of what could happen and then laughed at her first involuntary shudder.

At night when he claimed her roughly and took his pleasure with her, she would lie unresponsive, willing herself to remain unmoved. But it was a challenge for him and each time her own passionate nature betrayed her. Each morning she awakened with a sense of shame.

I'll kill him some day, was her comforting thought, then she bleakly wondered how that would happen. If she was lucky enough to hide a knife and stick it in his ribs, she would be at the mercy of those dirty stinking men and they would use her until she died.

She ground her teeth in her inner rage.

But perhaps in the boy there was hope. She soon noticed that El Condor rarely left the camp except when a dangerous sortie was to be made and then it was conducted in a military fashion, as she could see by the way they left the camp, which made Lucia wonder if El Condor had once been in the army.

It was Julio who headed the bunch when they went about their business. She already knew there were look-outs posted on each side of the gap leading out of their mountain retreat. She also knew that on these occasions, El Condor would climb up to his own look-out and scan the mountain ranges for enemy movement. It seemed that El Condor expected and waited for a force to come up against him. Or was it retribution because of the eerie strains of a trumpet which resounded and echoed around the mountain ranges? What significance had it for El Condor and why, when he heard it, would he turn to drink?

Lucia concluded that El Condor was a very unhappy man, haunted and walking on the edge of a bottomless pit of his own making.

It was most puzzling.

Now she watched him walk with firm steps to their hut. His face showed no hint of concern that he'd just shot two men in the back. He kicked the door open and eyed her, his eyes hard.

'You saw nothing, you heard nothing. Right?'

She nodded, keeping the rough wooden table between them.

'Good. Now get out, you distract me and I have work to do!' He reached for a pen and a clean sheet of paper and she wondered what his work could be,

41

but she moved sideways past the table and out of the open door, thankful to be so dismissed. Obviously his mind was not on love but something else.

She looked back once and saw that he was making a crude drawing that looked like a map. Perhaps he was plotting another raid, and her hopes grew high. If he left the camp with his men, then she might put a plan of her own in action.

She wandered aimlessly about the camp, keeping well away from the men surrounding the fire. They were drinking and talking softly to each other. They were subdued and they needed drink to boost their morale for had the brothers not been lively and entertaining, good singers, and their *amigos*?

It was a dirty business, and now the brothers were planted underground.

Lucia passed the youth, whose eyes followed her. He was humping a huge bale of last year's meagre hay to a row of horses tied to a long lariat in a makeshift corral. On impulse she followed him.

The hay smelled musty and she sneezed. He smiled as she rubbed her suddenly wet nose on the back of her wrist.

'The hay, it is dusty,' he said shyly, 'you must stand back or it will get into your throat, *señora*.'

'How about you? Does it not affect you?'

He shrugged. 'I am used to it. I pinch my nostrils thus.' He turned to her, his mouth pulled down and his nose taking on a pinched look. 'I also hold my breath.'

The resulting grimace made her laugh. He

reminded her of a monkey she'd once seen. He laughed with her and he seemed less shy.

'What is your name? What should I call you?'

At once he looked frightened and peered both ways to see if they were being watched. He let out a deep breath when he saw the men around the fire were still talking seriously.

'Pepe. I have no other name, just Pepe but you mustn't call me that,' he finished with a rush. 'El Condor does not like his prisoners to become friendly with anyone.'

'There have been many?'

Pepe lifted sad eyes to her and nodded slowly.

'They come and go. I think some are held to ransom, and others . . .' he shook his head, 'I don't know.' He stared into the distance and then said softly, 'There was once a young *señorita*, a child . . . she cried much, it hurt me here,' and he put a hand on his heart. 'She tried to run away and El Condor beat her, and then she disappeared.'

'You think he killed her?'

But Pepe turned away and then said softly,

'I don't know what happened. I just don't know. She was pretty, you know.'

He moved down the row of animals and shook out hay for each one.

'Pepe?'

'*Sí, señora?*'

'If there is a chance . . . would you help me to escape?'

He looked at her long and consideringly.

'It would mean death for me, *señora*, if El Condor found out I helped you. He is as the bird of prey who flies overhead. He sees and hears all. They say at night when the moon is full he changes into a condor and flies over the mountains and seeks out his enemies.'

'But that is nonsense! No man can do that!'

'But how is it he knows everything everyone does?'

Lucia was nonplussed. Did El Condor know everything?

'He must have many spies. . . .' She finished uncertainly. It wasn't possible for him to turn into a huge bird, for God's sake!

Pepe suddenly looked sly. Again he looked all around him to see that no one was watching.

'But I know something he doesn't know!' he said a little smugly.

'Oh? And what is that?'

'It's a secret and if I tell you it won't be a secret any more.'

'Come on, Pepe. You can trust me. I wouldn't even tell El Condor what day it is!'

He looked stubborn.

'I shouldn't have spoken.'

'But you have and I know that you know something El Condor doesn't know. If I kiss you, Pepe, will it loosen your tongue?'

She held her breath. Would the hope of a kiss work? She was sure Pepe had little carnal knowledge of women in general. She waited.

He looked at her uncertainly. Was she joking? She was an old woman compared to him. He'd never kissed a young girl, never mind an experienced woman. He began to tremble. He licked his lips and his eyes fastened on her mouth and Lucia saw and licked her own lips, her tongue protruding, enticing.

He gave a gulp, his adam's apple popping up and down. There was a sensation in his trousers. Holy Mother of God, she was doing things to him with only the suggestion of a kiss!

'Hide behind the horse here. She's quiet.' His voice was thick and croaky. Lucia smiled to herself. Poor boy. He was a virgin with very little chance of meeting girls. She resolved to give him such a kiss, he'd never forget it in his lifetime. It would become the kiss to compare with all others. . . .

She thrust out her breasts and opened her arms to him. He felt the sensation of being smothered in warm pulsing flesh as her arms closed about him. He breathed in her womanly scent and became weak at the knees. She was holding him up and then her full ripe lips fastened on his, which sent his senses swirling.

His mouth was forced open and he felt the caressing tingling sensation as her tongue probed his mouth. He wanted it to go on for ever as his excitement grew and he exploded in his trousers.

She was cradling him like the baby he was, and his whole being was concentrated on mouth and crotch.

Surprisingly, she was enjoying it too. She felt an over-whelming sense of power over him. He would be her slave. . . .

Then it was over. Reluctantly his lips were torn away from hers. Both were panting. He felt weak and wanted to sink to the ground. Nothing in his life had prepared him for what had happened.

'Now tell me your little secret,' she said softly, and afterwards I shall reward you with another kiss!'

He trembled at the thought of another such kiss. The words tumbled from him.

'The Americano who plays the trumpet is my friend. I know where he lives, but El Condor does not!' he finished triumphantly.

She didn't believe him.

'You're lying, Pepe. How could you know the trumpet-man?'

Pepe looked hurt.

'I am not lying, *señora*. It is true. I am his friend. One day I was sent out into the mountains to look for El Condor's favourite horse which had broken his halter and gone after a bunch of wild mustangs. He was a stallion you see and smelled a mare in heat. I was climbing up a ridge to look into another valley to see if I could see the herd. I slipped and rolled a long way down the other side and finished up on a narrow ledge. I was frightened. I have no head for heights and I was nervous even looking over the ridge. I was there all night, not daring to move.'

'Poor you. It must have been a dreadful ordeal.'

'It was. I prayed to the Virgin all night. I knew if I slept I should roll off the edge. I had to stay awake and the Virgin helped me.'

'Then what happened?'

'I heard sounds. Rocks were being dislodged and to my right there was a steep crag where birds flapped and hovered and I was surprised to see someone climbing amongst them with a bag on his back. It was the Americano and he was collecting birds' eggs. I shouted many times before he heard me and then he looked around and waved, and soon he came and threw me a rope but I dared not try to climb. I cried, and he fastened the rope to a pinnacle of rock and climbed down to me.' He sighed and shuddered. 'I shall never forget that climb and the relief I felt, when he'd bullied and shouted at me and told me where to find foot- and hand-holds, and I finally reached the top. I lay and sobbed and he slapped my cheeks and told me to pull myself together. Then he cracked several of his eggs one by one and made me drink until I told him I couldn't hold any more. Then he took me to his hideout in the mountains and we talked and I told him that I lived in the camp with El Condor and was out hunting his stallion.'

'Did you find the horse?'

'Yes, the Americano knew where the herd were feeding. He was very interested to know where the camp was. I told him. Then we parted and I found

47

the stallion and took him back to camp. I never told El Condor what happened.'

'And afterwards?'

'I have seen the Americano many times. I hear his music which is usually very sad and I know when he is troubled because he always sounds the reveille, playing over and over again before finishing with the last post. He is a haunted man, *señora*.'

Lucia considered him. This simple boy couldn't make up all that. It must be true.

'Would he help me to escape, Pepe?'

Pepe looked surprised. He'd never thought of asking the Americano to do anything for him. He would surely help a woman . . . wouldn't he?

He looked about him again, fearful, and saw Luc getting up to leave the group of men. He was coming towards them and unbuttoning his flies as he came.

'Next time I see him, I'll ask. I can do no more, *señora*,' he muttered as he moved away. 'Stay hidden until all is clear. Luc is coming.' Drooping his shoulders he moved on to run his hands down the next horse's near fetlock. But he needn't have worried. Luc was in a hurry and his mind was on relieving himself.

Gradually Lucia made the rounds of the camp and this time she was studying the hills and gaps and how the stream tumbled its way down into the valley below. She realized then that there was only the one way out and it was guarded on both sides by watchers who could see far beyond what she could see.

She bit her lip. To escape she would have to climb upwards beyond the snowline. The air at camp level was thin. Moving hurriedly brought on gasping chest pains, so climbing upwards was out.

Her only hope was Pepe and if it pleased the good Lord, the Americano would help her.

There was no one to report her missing. Her own family was far away and expecting her to be cared for in the da Silva family, and as for her stepson, he would be pleased if she was dead.

She shivered. She was alone in the world and only her courage and wit could help her now.

Four

Ben Jackson settled himself in his look-out position preparing for a long watch. He wore part of an old grey army blanket as a poncho, with a hole in the middle for his head. It blended in with the surrounding rocks. Keeping totally still, he knew he had little chance of being detected by any guards around the camp.

This was the camp the boy referred to, he guessed. There couldn't be so many camps up in these mountains.

He was a little outside his own territory. He'd been following the tracks of a bunch of men who'd killed his wolfhound and each time he thought of Snapper's agonizing death, his anger flared. Poor old Snapper, his friend and companion for the last seven years had had a lot of life in him, if he hadn't been netted by those bastards, muzzled and hung up to a bough of a tree by a hind leg, along with a young lynx; the two had clawed each other to death.

No doubt the turd-eating bastards thought it a rare sport.

He sat hunched up, the long-distance Spencer repeating rifle for which he'd swopped many skins at the trading post, beside him. He sat figuring how to do the most damage to the men in the camp. Granted he didn't know which of the lounging men below were responsible. It was enough to know that whoever they were, they were down there.

He wished he had army field-glasses, so that he could study the men's faces. But it was enough to sit and watch.

The group of lean-to and crazy shanties were a miserable sight, for there was rubbish strewn around. He could make out a pile of bones and a tip for other rubbish. The smell seemed to waft upwards on the wind. There was a privy too, standing alone, and now and again one of the men would visit it. Ben gauged the distance. It would be easy with the Spencer at that distance to take one of them in the heart. But that would only be one. It wasn't enough.

Suddenly he frowned. An authoritative figure had appeared at the door of the largest hut. He strode forward with a military bearing and the men lounging around the fire sprang to attention as if called to parade.

There was something familiar about the man. It was his walk as he strode up and down haranguing the men. He was bare-headed with a wealth of grey-white hair, and though broad in the shoulder, a slight

51

paunch gave the impression of a man going to seed, who didn't get enough exercise to keep him hard fit. A man who liked the good things of life.

As he watched, Ben saw two men break ranks and go for their horses and mount up. They rode off at a gallop towards what Ben considered the only way out of the small valley.

Ben wondered what orders they'd been given and it was with a state of shock he saw the leader deliberately reach for his rifle, take aim and fire. The bastard was good too. Both men took the bullets in the back.

Ben let his breath out in a gasp. Jesus!

Then it came to him. He remembered. The mutterings and the whispers about the man they called El Condor. This wasn't any old camp of outlaws. This was the camp of the most vicious outfit in Mexico!

His eyes turned again to the man known as El Condor and again, he felt that feeling of 'knowing'. He narrowed his eyes and stared hard. What if that man had curly black hair? Would he know him then?

Then it came to him like a punch in the belly. The man down below was General Santa Anna's lickspittle dogsbody, Coronel Fernandez, the hated officer whose stentorian voice could be heard roaring, 'No prisoners, damn you! The order is no prisoners to be left alive!'

That was the time when Ben last saw his father, wounded who yet could think of Ben's safety.

'Hide boy! Get you down into the cesspit and stay there until all is over. Go!' and he'd staggered away. Ben had watched him look back once and wave him away.

Ben's mind always blanked out the next hours when he'd plunged down into the thick cloying depths of the stinking sewer, the grating overhead and the sky above gradually turning from blue to blackness, the coming of the dawn and he, more dead than alive crawling out of that devil's hole and finding a sickening stillness and only the hum of flies to be heard.

Those memories when they did rise up from the void of his mind were the stuff of nightmares and it was then that the urge to play the trumpet overcame him. The trumpet-calls to arms were for him a call to the spirits of those dead comrades, to assure them that they were not forgotten and that some day he would have his revenge.

Now his heart beat fast. Perhaps that day was coming on apace when the revenge he'd longed for would happen. Maybe God had taken Snapper as payment for the chance to pay a debt. . . .

He slid away from his perch. This would take some thinking about. He was one man against many. He would have to have a plan.

Then his eye caught sight of a woman walking around the camp. A woman in that camp of no women? She walked slowly and deliberately and put him in mind of a prowling cat. She must be a prisoner. For a few minutes he watched her and she stopped to talk to a youth. Ben smiled. He recognized the youth as the one he'd befriended in the mountains. Maybe he would be the answer to his problem. . . .

Jeff Onslow prepared to mount up. He looked his gelding over with an experienced eye. He pulled at girths and saddle and checked his canteen and saw his saddle-bags and bedroll were well secured. He and his men were preparing for a long trail into the mountains and he was determined not to come back to this burnt-out defeated town until El Condor and his crazy bunch were wiped out once and for all time. They were a blight on the land.

Red Baines eyed him, smiling.

'Like old times, boss.'

Jeff nodded. 'Yeah, those were the days.' He glanced towards Wang. 'You think he can make it?'

'He's tough is Wang, and revenge will keep him alive.'

'That's how I figure him. What about the others?'

Red rasped his chin with a horny finger. He cast his eyes over the other men making their preparations.

'Apart from Ely, I wouldn't trust the sons of bitches with a dead cat!'

'Not even Carlos? He's my deputy.'

'Not even him. There's somethin' about him . . .'

'Yeah, I know what you mean ... something sly and smouldering underneath that toothy smile of his!'

Red nodded. 'You got it, boss. He bears watchin', that one!'

As well as Ely, Wang, Red and Carlos, there were six rather reluctant volunteers who made up the posse. Two were town layabouts, persuaded by lump sums from the town coffers if and when El Condor and his outfit were either apprehended for trial or at least smoked out of their area for good. The other four men were in it for the cash, the love of the hunt, or a genuine interest in their town's welfare.

A mixed bunch, thought Jeff sourly, and God knows how they'll react if we come under serious fire. He hid his misgivings from his own men, known and trusted in battle. He could count on them.

The young Mexican in the rather florid dress of the *caballero* kneed his horse towards Jeff, the wide sombrero he sported supported at his back by a chin-strap, showing curly black hair now shaggy and down to his shoulders. A gold ring gleamed in one ear, as did a gold tooth amongst a row of very white molars.

'*Señor*, I am known as Tijuana.' He held out a hand to Jeff. Jeff noted it was firm and calloused along the forefinger. 'I am a stranger in these parts.' He grinned. 'Perhaps I should say I am not welcome back in Chihuahua. A matter of honour, you know. Someone took my woman ...' He shrugged. 'I punished them both. You understand, *señor*?'

Jeff grunted.

'What you did is none of my business, as long as you can handle a gun!'

Tijuana laughed and with a sudden smooth practised movement, pulled his gun and aimed at a passing bird. It exploded into a mass of feathers which floated gently to the ground.

The report startled the horses. They lunged and nickered and some of the men who were still arranging their knapsacks cursed and swore as they hung on to reins as feet kicked out and tails swished.

'What the hell. . . ?' roared Ely, 'What fool let off a gun amongst these here goddam hosses?'

Ely was a tough gristly old man but his deep throaty yell was just as strong as it was when he was a gunner sergeant.

Tijuana grinned and gave Ely a mocking wave.

'I am that fool, *señor*. I show the sheriff here that I am no stranger with a gun, I am a *caballero* and the best shot I know. I am still alive, yes? Do you want to challenge me? I am always ready to test my skill . . . against any man!'

Ely spat and looked the Mexican up and down. Tight fancy pants which must be uncomfortable for his balls, frilly shirt and short jacket covered in gold braid. Some target for a real mean gunslinger. He reckoned the young buck was just pissproud.

But Ely's eyes narrowed when he saw the businesslike pistols in the well-oiled twin holsters. They weren't new like his troubador get-up. They looked well used.

'You good with your left hand?'

'*Sí señor*, or I should not carry the weight of an extra pistol. You want me to show you?'

Ely shook his head hurriedly.

'No, might spook the horses again. I guess we'll have plenty of opportunities later for you to show what you can do.'

Ely glanced at Jeff who was raising his eyebrows and grinning.

'Now if you're all ready, we'll move out and see if we can get a line on those bastards!'

They made a small cavalcade. Carlos rode as guide in front of Jeff Onslow. Despite being a drunken layabout, he knew the surrounding terrain. When indignant townsfolk lost patience with him and refused to give him handouts, he would go hunting mountain cats for skins and small animals for meat. He knew many secrets of the mountains.

His lips hinted at a smile as they rode ahead. Jeff glanced at him and wondered what was cooking in that devious brain.

'Where is the most likely place to start looking?' Jeff asked him now.

Carlos shrugged. 'We can but follow what tracks they made until they hit the hard rocky ground. After that, it will be luck.'

Jeff was despondent. The early trail had petered out. All they could do was move on in the direction the outfit had taken.

The going was rough and as they entered the foothills, the rocks grew into boulders and the streams of water seen like narrow snail-trails seemed to disappear completely. Looking about him, Jeff saw that Carlos was leading them into the desert.

'Look, you do know what you're doing?' Jeff asked dubiously after several hours of riding and not seeing a living thing except a condor with a twelve-foot span wheeling and flapping as it prepared to land on its huge nest perched high on a promontary.

'*Sí*. I have been this way many times. It is good country for catching the big cats . . . the cougars . . .'

'Yes, yes, but we're not hunting cougars, we're looking for signs of a camp. Have you never seen smoke from camp-fires or travellers of any sort? No prospectors looking for silver, or sheepherders or anyone?'

'Oh, yes, *señor*. Many times, but they are local peasants not bad Comancheros who perhaps trade with the Indians.'

'You think El Condor trades with the Indians?'

'Of course, or why would he hide out in these parts? He robs banks in Texas for cash for his men but he also robs trains, yes? That is for goods, *señor*. It is well known that he pays for those who spy for him in goods, or why would the peons help him?'

'Hmm. So the villagers in this region will not tell us the truth when we ask for news of El Condor?'

Carlos shook his head.

'It will be better not to ask. That way they will not

be on their guard. If we come upon a village it would be better to please the local tavern-keeper by buying beer and treating the locals. That way you can loosen tongues.'

'And a good excuse for you to get a skinful!'

Carlos grinned. 'It is as the good God wills! I am a good Catholic and God forgives all good Catholics even such as I!'

Jeff snorted. 'I'll not be so forgiving if we don't get a smell of that bastard. You'll find yourself behind bars again mighty quick for not doing your duty!'

'What can a man do, but his best?'

'Well, at the moment your best is not good enough. Now let's camp by that pool yonder and have an early start in the morning.'

Carlos whistled as he unloaded his horse and helped set up camp under a stand of scrawny trees. The wind, as the sun went down, was becoming cold. A fire was expertly built with dried moss and small sticks, and when the flames licked up dry deadwood was skilfully placed on top. Soon there was a pleasant warmth and when the men had eaten and Ely's old coffee-pot had sent forth the smell of bubbling coffee, the men sat back and relaxed.

Tijuana drew a mouth-organ from inside his shirt and played some lively Mexican airs, then as the men clapped, danced a jig, his feet tapping to his music. Tijuana had suddenly become popular.

But the music ceased when the faint strains of a trumpet resounded around the distant hills.

Tijuana looked around at the others. For a moment sheer superstition shone from his eyes. The mouth-organ dropped from his fist and a gun took its place.

'*Madre de Dios!* What is that?' Jeff reached out, slapping down the gun so it pointed to the ground.

'Careful, *amigo*. That's no spirit. Just a man playing a trumpet.'

'He sounds like a haunted spirit.' Tijuana looked pale and shaken. 'Are you sure it's some *hombre* and not one of those phantom soldiers lost at the Alamo?'

Carlos laughed a high drunken laugh. He held up the remains of a bottle of tequila.

'Take a drink, *amigo*. Your imagination will make you piss your tight pants. The massacre at the Alamo was thirty years ago! Even ghosts in limbo will have found their way to the afterworld by now! What kind of prancing puppy are you?'

Tijuana's eyes glittered with fury.

'Some day I shall show you what kind of puppy I am! Listen! Whoever is out there, is tormented. He sends out a message. Can't you understand. Whether a man or a ghost, he is warning that he is there watching, like some predator biding his time, waiting for the right moment!'

'Hark at him! Is he some kind of oracle, with a gift for probing a man's mind? He is but a crazy man who plays a trumpet to amuse himself!' But Carlos's brave words didn't hide the uneasiness at the back of his eyes.

Jeff noted the uneasiness and again wondered what secret lay behind the usually smiling face.

The trumpet ceased its call abruptly. There was a sinister chill and everyone listening held his breath. Would the mad trumpeter start up again?

The other men muttered amongst themselves.

'It's a bad sign,' one of the men said softly. 'That one up there watches everything and everyone. I met a goatherder once who swore that he knows when storms are brewing and crops are going to fail. I say the man's a devil and should be hunted down!'

'And then what?' asked another man.

'I dunno. String him up or run him across the river into Texas, but get rid of him somehow. There's those that say he watches everything going on in the mountains and he's got the evil eye.'

'Hell! You've got as much imagination as Tijuana!'

'I tell you it's true! Once, he was seen watching a meeting between El Condor's man Julio and Chief Lone Wolf of the Mescaleros. They were dickerin' over guns. All seemed well, with a bargain struck, and then, when El Condor gave the signal for the rest of the consignment in two wagons to come out from their hiding place,the two wagons's brakes failed and horses and wagons were dragged downhill and tumbled into the gorge below. Goddammit, not one gun or horse was saved! It was him, that skulkin' Americano with the evil eye. He made it happen!'

The listeners looked at the man curiously. Carlos

spat.

'How come you know so much?'

'It was told to me by a man I drink with. He swore it was true.'

'Maybe the brakes would have failed even if that feller hadn't been watchin'.'

'Well, all I know is that El Condor's man was mighty mad and the chief backed off and before you could say, What's yours? the whole dang lot of 'em had disappeared into the pass. Those Indians knew somethin' and to them it was bad medicine.'

Jeff now intervened. He thought the discussion had gone on long enough.

'Right, you lot. Get bedded down. We move out at dawn.'

Jeff couldn't sleep. He felt spooked. It was as if they were all being watched and followed. He'd not felt right ever since they'd started out. He'd put it down to Carlos and his superstitions but perhaps it was something else, an instinct for danger that had developed during the war.

He threw back his blanket, got up and stretched. He'd go for a walk and have a cigarette.

Red Baines stirred. 'You awake too, boss? Is it that feller buggin' you?'

Red also got up and the two men walked with catlike tread to the perimeter of the camp. They walked towards the line of horses tethered along a rawhide rope. They all appeared quiet and sleeping.

All was quiet, too quiet. Not even a mouse stirred.

Jeff lit a cigarette and offered his pack to Red who took one. For a few minutes they stood quietly enjoying the smoke.

'What you think about this trumpet-blowing American, Red? D'you think he'll be a danger to us? He's certainly not one of El Condor's men or why would he be spyin' on them?'

'Some crazy-in-the-head guy with bees buzzin' between his ears. Probably some loco prospector sufferin' from a fall of rock. There's a lot of 'em about in the hills.'

'Tijuana's dangerous. He could have caused a stampede back to San Antonio. I wouldn't give a fart for those so-called volunteers. I guess I'll be relying on you and Ely and Wang for what we do.'

Red hesitated and then spoke his mind.

'You sure we ain't takin' on too much, boss? There's a whole heap of El Condor's men and if we find their hang-out, we'll have the devil's own job to shift them!'

Jeff grinned.

'I've got an ace in the hole, Red. I wasn't for blabbin' it to all those sons of bitches. But I gotta clutch of eggs in my saddle-bags, left over from the war . . .'

'You mean. . . ?' Red's eyes gleamed.

Jeff nodded. 'Yeah. Li'l old grenades. I always reckoned they'd come in useful sometime.'

'Why, you sly sonofabitch!' Red said admiringly. 'You sure do think ahead!'

'Why d'you think I was fool enough to take a job like this? We'd never shift those swine with rifles and hand-guns. They might even have cannon stashed up in them there mountains.'

Red looked serious.

'I never thought of that. Hell! It could be like war all over again!'

'You think the worst, Red, and then you'll be prepared. I'm gonna talk like a father to those guys in the mornin' and put it straight. Anyone with a yeller spine and no balls can get to hell out of it. Those eggs mean the difference of having an army with us, or us goin' in as an assault team.'

'By God, you planned it this way, didn't you?'

'Sort of. I reckon once we locate the bastards, we use those half-inch townies as bait. Four of 'em should be enough. They can cause a diversion. We keep Tijuana with us. He's a gunman but we've yet to find out his potential. Anyhow, he's a mad bastard and I'd rather he was with us than riskin' any trouble with the others.'

'How we go about it, boss?'

'I'll tell you better when we find out their location. We'll have to do a recce as we did in the war. Remember? Find the weakest points and work it out from then on.'

'What about that feller up there?' Red indicated the hills behind him.

'We keep our eyes skinned as we go. That's all we can do. Now come on, let's hit the hay. It'll soon be mornin'.'

The men listened grim-faced as Jeff spelled out the danger. But he was wrong about the yellow spines and lack of balls. None of them wanted to turn back and Jeff felt a sense of relief.

They broke camp and moved on, climbing higher into the mountains. The air grew cold and thin. The men shivered and grumbled but carried on. It was late afternoon after a midday break for hot coffee and slices of cold meat and hunks of bread, when they saw the wisp of smoke rising straight up into a sparkling sunlit sky. Red nodded and drew Jeff's attention to it.

'What you make of that, boss? You reckon it's Indians or some prospector or could it be that there camp we're huntin' up?'

Jeff studied the smoke through his glasses and then handed them to Red.

'Too much smoke for a prospector. It's the wrong time of day for a lone man to eat. It's not Indian smoke. They don't use green wood unless they're on a talkin' jag and then the smoke goes up in puffs. No, that's comin' from a big white man's camp, I reckon. What you think?'

Red studied the smoke and what he could see of the surrounding terrain. He reckoned the smoke was some ten or fifteen miles away as the crow flies. God knows how long it would take for them to come up with it. There could be many hazards ahead. He gave the glasses back to Jeff.

'You could be right, boss. What do we do now? Make a forced march and get as near as we can before daylight?'

'I reckon.'

Red turned in his saddle and waved to the men coming up behind them. He pointed to the smoke.

'We're gonna press on, fellers and check out that smoke. We think it could be the camp we're lookin' for.'

Wang kneed his horse closer.

'You want for me to go on ahead, boss? Me get close like snake in grass. One man make less noise than many men.'

Jeff looked at him consideringly. Wang had lost weight since the death of his son and the girl. His face was like a yellow skull. He sensed a death wish in the old man.'

'Only if you take someone with you, Wang, old pal. It's new country out there. Two of you could perhaps do it.'

Wang shook his head.

'Me no fool. Not wish to go to ancestors yet. I move like demon ghost. Same way as we did when spying on Yankees!'

'But those Yankees were rookie soldiers with little experience of trackers and trackin'. These bastards' survival instincts are finely honed. They live like animals scentin' danger. They will be much more aware. No, if you go, someone goes with you!' His tone was firm and authoritative and Wang shook his head despondently.

'I wish my son was still alive. He and I worked well together. Woe is me! My heart is heavy!'

Tijuana nudged his horse forward and looked Jeff straight in the eyes. He was serious.

'I shall go with him. I shall look after the old man!'

Jeff wanted to laugh. It was ludicrous! Someone look after Wang? He was small and light but when his fighting spirit was aroused, he was a veritable tiger. Probably he would end up looking after Tijuana!

'Very well,' Jeff answered and it took all his control not to laugh. 'You look out for Wang. I leave him in your care!'

Wang gave Jeff a venomous look, if one could call an inscrutable face and flashing eyes a venomous look. He turned to Tijuana,

'If you come with me, load up now. I am ready to leave now. We eat later.'

'Hey now, *amigo*, just a minute . . .'

'I say, hurry, greasy Mex or I shall leave you behind!'

Five

El Condor looked at the scene of devastation at Sanderson's Halt. The train was standing idle, black smoke belching from its chimney, the driver and fireman's corpses hanging askew from their cabin. On each side of the train several passengers lay where they'd been shot as they'd tried to flee the attack. But most of the bodies were of uniformed soldiers, the guard who were protecting the payroll for Fort Stockton.

Two of his men were heaving the heavy chest on to the military reinforced wagon. That alone was worth the raid. The four horses were strong and well fed. Most useful. The soldiers waiting for the payroll were all dead. With luck they would be clean away before the alarm sounded at the Fort.

Other men searched the victims for money and other valuables. He saw Julio humping foodsacks on to the buckboard. Good old Julio, always thinking of his belly.

He felt elated. It was another blow for the hated military. God damn those bastards in Mexico City for hounding him out of the army! The hypocritical swine, Santa Anna, who used him and then turned on him, giving him no support! He spat. It angered him and made his brains boil whenever he was reminded of him.

Now, the elation in him fed his sense of power. His were the brains and the imagination to plan and oversee each operation to its final outcome. His men needed him, worshipped him.

Worshipped? Maybe not worshipped but regarded him with awe. Never had they lived so well, felt so free as in the mountains, enjoyed the plentiful women and no restrictions of their carousing between raids. They were content . . . or he thought they were.

He thought of Lucia da Silva and felt the gold cross and chain in his vest pocket. He had wrested it from the neck of a dead nun. Not that he would tell her how he'd got it. Suffice to know that he thought well of her. She might even be grateful and give her favours voluntarily. He was getting a little weary about fighting for what he got.

At first it was exciting, the challenge to tame her, but he wasn't a young man any longer. He wanted a woman to be exciting but compliant too. Lucia was like trying to bed a mountain cat. The cross should do the trick.

Suddenly he was startled by the train's hooter blowing.

He looked up and saw that the driver, whom he'd thought dead, was leaning over his controls, pulling the hooter cord, his head drooping on his chest.

All the men looked up from their various activities. All looked towards him for orders. He waved an arm, pointing to the distant hills. They knew what it meant. They had to be away before someone came looking for the train.

He raised his hand-pistol, took careful aim and felt the kick-back of the gun as the bullet took the driver in the brain.

The eerie *woo-hooing* of the hooter ceased abruptly and only the engine's escaping steam could be heard. Julio threw on the last sack of flour on to the well-laden wagon, climbed up, took the reins and with a yell stroked the right leader with the whip hooked in his boot. The team moved ahead slowly, got into stride and with a giddy-up from Julio, picked up a fast pace, the rest of the men following.

They left two men behind, shot early on during the raid. It was regrettable but all knew the risks taken.

It was a wild punishing ride for both men and horses. The army wagon lurched and bumped over the uneven ground as Julio's wild whooping urged the sweating horses on.

But they had good start. It would take days for the military to get on their trail and, travelling over hard, stony ground, they would leave no clear trail.

It would take more than a trained army-scout to follow them deep into Mexico. . . .

*

Lucia da Silva watched the men leave the camp. She watched as the guards squatting above the narrow inlet to the small valley waved their rifles in encouragement to their comrades. So there were still men placed at intervals around the camp. El Condor was taking no chances, she thought, grinding her teeth.

Two guards could cause havoc if a small hostile party found its way into the valley, and she, on her own, had no chance of escaping. Even if she had got past the guards, she would not be able to find her way in those hills, and the piercing cold at night would kill her.

She saw Pepe watching the little cavalcade move out. He was carrying a bucket of kitchen waste. Not for him the thrill of going on a raid. He was regarded as an idiot, only good enough to do the dirtiest jobs in the camp and bullied unmercifully by the bad-tempered cook who got roaring drunk each night after serving up the muck he called stew. Pepe put him to bed and cleaned up his vomit.

Lucia wondered how Pepe could stand such a miserable life. Once, when she'd asked him, he'd shrugged his shoulders and said sulkily that it was better than being an outcast. At least he got his belly filled.

Now she saw him watching her. Her heart leapt. Maybe he was remembering that she'd asked for his help. Casually she strolled across to him.

'Where's your boss?'

Pepe grinned. 'Lying on his bed with a bottle of tequila. Says that if anyone wants to eat tonight they can fix their own. When El Condor's away, the fat pig says it's fiesta time for him!'

'Pepe . . . remember I asked you . . .' she stopped as Pepe looked guilty, peering here and there to see if curious eyes were on them. The camp was quiet but it was not entirely deserted. El Condor always left a skeleton crew on the alert for any emergency.

'I'm sorry, *señora*, I cannot . . . I dare not help you! It would mean my life. El Condor would read my mind. He would *know* I helped you . . . I cannot. Do not ask me!'

'Have you talked with the man with the trumpet? Would you go to him and ask him to come?'

Pepe shivered and turned away, muttering and crossing himself.

'El Condor is a devil. You are his woman and the one who helps her to escape would not suffer a bullet in the head. It could mean many hours of torture. I have seen what El Condor can do to those who enrage him!'

'Pepe, listen! I asked you if you'd seen the man with the trumpet. That's all I want to know.'

Pepe blinked and looked at her.

'Yes, he knows you are here. He has seen you many times. I told him you are held against your will but he just sits up there stroking and polishing his trumpet and waiting.'

'Waiting for what?'

Pepe shrugged. 'Who knows how a *hombre* touched by God thinks? I only think he waits. Or why should he sit up there on the crag, watching?'

They both looked upwards to the range of hills that seemed to brood in the sun. Dark, rocky prominences with little foliage even for wild goats, which spelled danger to all who roamed there.

'Does he sit there every day?'

'Not all the time. He moves around, but that high peak over there is his favourite place. That is where he plays his music and El Condor curses him for coming back to haunt him.'

'You think the music is a threat to El Condor?'

Pepe's strange, sometimes vacant eyes lit up with an instinctive knowledge that sometimes an idiot can sense when no one else can tune in.

'*Sí, señora.* I have seen the fear surround him like an aura. I have smelled it. He does not think the trumpeter is human. He thinks . . .' Then he stopped abruptly and looked at Lucia and then muttered something about his tongue running away with him. 'You will think I'm a fool,' he finished and turned to walk away.

'Pepe, please . . . help me. Come with me. Help me to get away and I'll look after you. Take me to the man with the trumpet. Please.'

Pepe turned back to her, now uncertain.

'You mean I should become part of your family?'

'Yes . . . yes! I will help you. You can start a new life!'

'But this is the only life I know. These hills are my home. I love the freedom . . .'

'But you're not free, Pepe! You are forced to fetch and carry for that horrible man. You clean him up and put him to bed and all you get for it is a beating if you don't please him. Don't you want a better life?'

Pepe gave her a long considering glance that was both sly and fatalistic.

'It is my life as I know it, *señora*, but could you make it different, or are you like all the others, just using and keeping poor Pepe quiet?'

'Oh, Pepe, am I in a position to use you? I just want you to help me and then I can help you!'

Pepe considered this, his simple mind working methodically, his dull face showing nothing of the tumult inside, the hope for a new future and the fear of El Condor.

Lucia felt like jumping up and down and shaking him in her impatience. Oh, God, if he didn't make his mind up soon, one of the guards would become curious as to why they were spending so much time together.

She looked around apprehensively, but none was in sight, due to El Condor's absence and their attitude that while the cat's away. . . .

Then Pepe slowly nodded. He'd come to a conclusion.

'I'll take you to the trumpet man, *señora*, and he will look after us both.'

'When? Should we go now?'

'Oh no. I've got the rest of the rubbish to get rid of . . .'

'Pepe, it doesn't matter about the rubbish! You're free of all that, don't you understand?'

Pepe looked about him fearfully.

'He'll kill me if I don't do as he says.'

Lucia shook him. Oh God, he was being difficult and wasting time. At any moment, one of the men could walk outside and stop them. She was in a ferment of agony. Dragging him reluctantly by the arm, she pulled him behind the nearest hut. Panting, she said through gritted teeth.

'Which way? Where do you get out? How do we find the trumpet man?'

The glazed look left Pepe's eyes. A direct question which he could answer brought his focus back. He pointed.

'Down behind the well. There's a cleft in the rock. It's an old watercourse.'

'Then what are we waiting for? Come on!'

Tijuana followed in Wang's footsteps. They had neared the campsite and if the faint scent of woodsmoke hadn't betrayed its presence, then the stench from the rubbish tip would have proclaimed human habitation.

Tijuana marvelled at the little man's ability to slide through the undergrowth without disturbing so much as a leaf. He felt himself to be big and clumsy,

75

like a buffalo crashing through vegetation, all over the place.

Wang had reproved him sharply and told him to go back and see to the horses if he couldn't move more quietly, and for a while Tijuana hardly dared breathe or put a foot down before him.

But he'd improved and now Wang was waving him on to belly up to the ridge and look down the great gully and into the valley below.

Wang motioned him to look to the right of him. He did so and saw two men squatting, one on each side of a gap in the hills, perched high. Only their movements had betrayed them. So this was El Condor's hideout.

He made out the faint track leading through the gap and using his field-glasses noted that this gap appeared to be the only outlet. It should be easy to block them in, once they were inside. Ranging his gaze over the quiet camp, he reckoned that the majority of the men must be out on a raid. Idly he wondered if El Condor was with them.

It would have been an ideal time to take the camp and ambush the returning men. But that was not to be. They had left Jeff Onslow too far away to get back and report and return in time.

Wang pulled at his arm and pointed. He focused on two small moving objects. Hell! A youth and a woman were climbing the steep crag far to the left of them and moving up fast. It was interesting to see that the woman had hitched up her skirts and she had a pair of damn fine legs.

Wang grinned up at him.

'You watch here for men's return, and I go and help woman.'

'No, old man, *you* stay and I help woman!' Grinning as well, Tijuana started to move along the ridge towards the two figures.

'*No!*' Wang's voice barked at him, stopping him in his tracks. '*You* stay here. You move like big wounded beast! I move like snake in the grass. I move quickly. You . . .' he shook his head, 'You have much to learn!'

'Why, you little yeller son of a bitch! I could squeeze you to death! I'll have you know I've got a reputation as a number one gunhawk! I can plug a man through the eye at fifty paces!'

'Sure, sure. . . .' Wang nodded his head until his pigtail swung up and down like a whip. 'Shooting gun no use in wilderness. All right in wild cow-town but here, want wild animal skill. Patience to stalk. You watch guards and for coming of El Condor and his men. Then you move fast, eh?'

Reluctantly, Tijuana watched Wang glide away and disappear into the undergrowth. Hell's fire! If it wasn't for the fact that the little yeller worm had lost a son, he'd string him up.

He watched and waited and hated it because the little man had given the order.

Wang moved at speed, his feet barely touching the ground. He didn't carry a gun but relied on a very sharp curved knife he'd brought from China when

77

he was a young boy. Around a shoulder and under one arm he carried a coil of rope. He was a wizard with rope and many an adversary had finished trussed up with rope burns in addition.

Now as he drew near where the sweating couple were climbing, he uncoiled his rope and looked over the ridge. The youth was climbing steadily and did not appear to be helping the woman.

Wang saw her resting, clinging on to tough bushes that had deep roots growing in crevices of rock. Head bent, she was panting. He knew she was nearly spent.

He gave a low whistle and both man and girl looked up in shock. He waved.

The youth gave a cry and nearly let go his hand-hold at the sight of the foreign yellow face, for Pepe thought a demon had come for him.

'Have no fear. I come to help you.'

Lucia, recognizing a Chinaman when she saw one, wondered whether he was the trumpet man. She didn't experience the fear that Pepe did.

Pepe wanted to scream and escape from the demon. But the only way he could do so would be to let go and hurtle down to the bottom of the cliff. Then of course, he would be at the demon's mercy if he was on the way to hell.

'Have mercy!' he yelled. 'All I've done is help this woman! I don't want to die!'

'Who talks of dying? I said I'm here to help. Here, catch rope. You climb easier.' Wang threw down his rope and Pepe's slow mind finally realized he was in no danger.

Wang wound the rope about a pinnacle of rock and then held on while Pepe climbed and at last heaved himself on to the ridge, gasping and weeping with the effort.

Then Wang went down the rope like a monkey swinging from a branch and gathered Lucia to him. He guided her hand- and footholds until both were safely on to firm ground beside Pepe.

Then they surveyed each other, Lucia and Pepe seeing a strange gnomelike figure with a yellow wizened face and black hair going grey, fastened back in a long plaited pigtail. He wore black shirt, loose over black canvas pants and boots that looked too big for him.

He saw a rather vacant boy and a white woman in some distress. He guessed that the woman had been El Condor's prisoner and maybe the youth too. They could be useful to Jeff Onslow.

He bowed.

'I am Wang. Who are you?'

Tijuana watched the three come towards him. He wasn't surprised at the little man's success. There was more about him than those who didn't know him realized. No wonder Jeff Onslow valued his friendship and ability.

He smiled at Lucia.

He liked the look of the woman despite the

ingrained dirt and dishevelled hair. She had curves in all the right places. . . .

Her eyes sparkled at the look of open appraisement. This man appreciated a woman. Lucia's heart lifted.

'I'm Lucia da Silva and this is Pepe.' She gestured to the youth standing by with head bowed. 'He helped me to escape from that lump of pigshit, El Condor, a devil in human form!' Her bosom heaved at the memory of the man and what she had endured at his hands. 'I hope his prick throbs with boils and blows up!' she finished with venom.

Tijuana flinched and then laughed.

'Ma'am, I don't know about his prick, but me and my friends aim to blow him up!'

Wang intervened.

'Come, no more talk. We go back to Jeff. She tell Jeff all she know about camp!'

Tijuana, feeling annoyed at Wang's interference, agreed. He'd been inclined to take things slowly, get to know the woman and the more he looked at her, the stronger the urge in his pants. He sighed. It would come later. He saw that certain look in her eyes. . . .

They turned and travelled towards Jeff's camp. Tijuana held Lucia in front of him and enjoyed her soft warmth, indulged in dreams of what was to come, while Pepe rode behind Wang, his black eyes and tense little figure on the watch for danger.

Wang eyed the Mexican gunman with contempt.

The fool would blunder into hell itself and not know it, all because he had a piece of prime woman near him! Wang spat on the ground. Everyone with sense put women in their rightful place and did not let them addle their minds. Tijuana would be an easy target for a bushwhacker.

Suddenly above them came the first clear notes of a trumpet. The long sweet tones played up and down the scale as if the player was flexing his fingers before readying himself for the real music.

Wang was off his horse in a flash and motioning to Pepe, said softly,

'Hold the horse and wait here.' Before Tijuana and Lucia guessed what he was about to do, he began to climb the escarpment. He climbed like a mountain goat, surefooted and with surprising strength in handholds.

He climbed swiftly and silently and only the sound of an occasional stone dislodged broke the natural sounds of wind and birds wheeling and calling.

The three below watched until Wang disappeared on to a ledge. The horses moved uneasily, reaching out to crop tufts of coarse grass. Tijuana's and Pepe's concentration was transferred to them, and all the while the music came in spurts.

Then a pistol shot rang out and the three below stiffened. Tijuana let out a long breath which he hadn't known he was holding.

'What in hell is happening up there?' He prepared to dismount. He felt a misgiving at tackling the escarpment, but if Wang needed help. . . .

Then Wang's yellow face appeared over the ridge and he was grinning and waving. Tijuana cupped his hands and shouted.

'You all right up there? What happened?'

Wang grinned again and pulled the trumpeter so that his face too was showing over the ridge. He looked dazed.

Then those below watched while Wang wrapped his rope about the trumpeter's shoulders and then pushed him over the edge.

They all gasped as the figure fell sharply for a few feet, then swung in the air, then gradually he came down until he lay in a heap before them.

Tijuana was off the horse and squatting beside the white man while Wang climbed down to come and stand beside them. Pepe shuffled forward, holding Wang's horse.

'Is he dead?' Pepe looked from one to the other.

Wang's face was now inscrutable.

'No. I could have killed him. He took a shot at me when he saw me, but I kicked him in the crotch and then knocked him out.'

'So, this is the elusive trumpeter.' Tijuana examined the man's features as far as he could under the rough black beard he sported.

He stank like a billy-goat, his clothes were rough and his jerkin was made of half-cured skins, but the trumpet, still fastened to his shoulder by a worn rawhide thong was highly polished and gleaming.

As Tijuana examined him, he opened his eyes. They were a bright blue, which startled Tijuana. At first they were vague and unfocused, then the man groaned and tried to sit up and the eyes grew keen.

'Goddamn that little yeller bastard! He kicked me in the balls!' He looked at Tijuana. 'Who the hell are you?' He rubbed himself carefully.

'It doesn't matter who I am. What's this with you frightening the *campesinos* half to death? Some folk think you're a ghost. What's with you, *señor*?'

'I live alone up there in the mountains. It's the only home I have. The music I play is the only pleasure I have. Can I help it if folk don't like it?'

'But it echoes around the mountains. You know what they say?'

'Of course. It keeps folk away.' Then he nodded at Pepe. 'He is my friend and that is the woman he wants me to take from El Condor.'

They all turned to look at Pepe who was standing smiling vaguely, waiting to be recognized. He nodded violently.

'*Sí.* He tells the truth. We meet sometimes and he plays his music for me. He is a good man. I know.'

Wang unwound the rope and Tijuana offered him his hip flask. Ben Jackson took a deep swallow. He didn't often get the chance of the good stuff. He usually brewed his own poison.

Tijuana looked at Wang.

'What do we do now?'

'Take him with us. What else?'

*

Coffee was brewing and the titillating smell of stew met the weary travellers when they entered the makeshift camp.

Jeff Onslow was waiting and he watched with surprise the three strangers coming with them. His eyes narrowed as he saw the hanging trumpet on the tramplike figure walking beside Tijuana's horse.

He helped Lucia da Silva off Tijuana's horse. She fell into his arms barely able to stand for the pains in her backside and legs.

'What happened, Tijuana?'

So the gunman filled him in. 'And so, boss, these three can give us good information about the camp.'

Jeff led Lucia to the camp-fire and lowered her to a blanket. Then, handing her a mug of black coffee, he asked gently, 'And how come you were in El Condor's camp?'

While he listened to Lucia, he studied the trumpet man, noting the lithe muscular body that denoted much climbing exercise. He took in the businesslike knife swinging at his hip, the old-fashioned rifle and the rough makeshift clothes he wore made from animal skins. A true backwoodsman.

Lucia told him bitterly about the raid and how El Condor had taken and used her and that even now he was away on some raid and was due back any time.

At that, his attention was taken from the man, who was now eating and drinking wolfishly with the idiot

84

boy, whom Jeff had passed over as harmless. He was just a bit of flotsam caught up in El Condor's machinations. But if what the woman said was true, they might still take El Condor by surprise.

His mind wandered to the old trail leading through the pass and into the high valley. El Condor's men would have to string out as only two horsemen could ride abreast, and a wagon would have little room to manoeuvre. . . .

He interrupted Lucia's flow of invective against El Condor.

'You there . . .' he squatted opposite Ben Jackson. 'Tell us who you are and why you play the trumpet. It's not for just pleasure, is it?'

Ben Jackson threw the dregs of his coffee away, picked up his trumpet and caressed it lovingly. He spoke slowly as if speech did not come easily to him.

'The trumpet is my friend, and my friend says all the things I feel inside of me and can't release myself. My father called me Ben, but that was a long time ago.'

'How long, Ben?' Jeff spoke softly, persuasively, knowing instinctively that Ben could dry up if the right words weren't spoken. Ben looked at him reflectively, eyes unnaturally bright with unshed tears.

'Thirty years.'

There was a long silence and Jeff racked his brains to come up with the proper approach.

'Thirty years. That must have been about the time

of the siege of the Alamo?' He held his breath. Had he been too outspoken?

Ben Jackson nodded and reached out for the coffee-pot and poured more coffee. Jeff drew a deep breath and waited, while Ben took a long gulp. Then he sighed and looked at Jeff and there was something haunted in his eyes. Jeff shivered at the lifetime's loneliness he saw there.

'I try not to think of the Alamo. It brings back memories. I was a lad and my pa was a sergeant. He made me hide in a sewer like some craven yellerbellied coward, which I was, and I heard the screams and shouts as all the survivors were butchered, my pa amongst them!'

Suddenly he was shaking and he put his head in his hands. 'I'll never forget the screams and the stench and the piercing cold and my guts turning to water! That is when my friend here,' he indicated his trumpet, 'takes over and I play and play, to give courage to the ghosts who still go on fighting!'

Sweat dripped from his forehead through his fingers. Jeff silently handed over his flask.

'Here, take a long swig, mister. It's the good stuff. It'll put new heart into you.'

Silently Ben did as he was told. His colour came back and his eyes lost their haunted look. He was once again facing reality. He looked at the others.

'So what are you doing out in these hills?'

'We're out to get El Condor and his men. They killed my friend's son and his woman.' Jeff indicated

Wang who'd been sitting and listening impassively to Ben. 'He is also wanted in Texas. The bastard has become too bold. He thinks he can cross the river any time he likes and get away with it. There's a big reward for El Condor and all his men. We aim to claim it.'

Ben nodded.

'I want El Condor too. He was Santa Anna's right-hand man, the infamous Coronel Fernandez. I saw him and it was the face in all my nightmares! Coronel Fernandez is El Condor!'

'That figures,' Tijuana said quietly as he listened to the tale. 'There was a great scandal after Santa Anna became president of Mexico, and Fernandez was drummed out of the Council. He thought he should have been Santa Anna's top aide and it didn't come off. He was lucky to escape with his life.'

'So that's the secret of why he's lasted so long. He treats his men as a military brigade,' Jeff said. 'They're all seasoned fighters and El Condor has all the military skills for planning his raids. So what are we going to do about him?'

He looked around at the others. Ely Johnson spat on the ground and pointed with his thumb at Lucia.

'They all rode out on a raid, if she's telling the truth.'

'She is,' confirmed Ben. 'I watched them ride out and they had enough equipment to go on a long haul. They were heading north.'

'So you reckon they won't be back for another day, maybe two?'

Ben nodded. 'I reckon. Maybe he can tell us something.' He nodded at Pepe who looked frightened at being the centre of attention. He shook his head violently.

'I only know they were going on a raid, *señors*. I watched them ride out and then the *señora* persuaded me to leave . . .' his voice broke. 'She promised to look after me.'

'And I will, Pepe, I will.' Lucia smiled at him putting her hand in his.'

Jeff leaned forward.

'Pepe, do you know any secret ways into that camp? Ways that only you know? Private places that maybe you go when you're unhappy?'

Pepe's eyes gleamed.

'There are such places. They think I'm stupid, but I know things they don't know, and I'm smart enough to keep my own secrets.' He looked pleased with himself. 'I can take you to places that even he doesn't know about.' He indicated Ben.

'Then will you do that, Pepe? and I'll give you a golden eagle.'

Pepe's eyes bulged. 'A golden eagle? I've heard of them but never seen one. I'll show you all the places. After all, I'll never see them again.' Now his tone was forlorn. It would hurt to leave the only home he'd ever known, even if those around him had treated him roughly and with contempt.

They decided the camp was safe and so Tijuana, Lucia and Ely rested up along with Red Baines and the volunteers, while Jeff and Wang, led by Ben and Pepe, geared up for a longer foray into the camp itself.

Checking guns and ammunition and supplies, they set off on foot, making good time as Ben led them through short cuts, across streams and up small canyons until Jeff and Wang were bewildered.

But Ben knew the terrain and sooner than they expected they were all looking down on to the camp below. In the far distance could be seen the meandering trail to the only gap into the valley. They were now at the opposite end of the small secret valley and in a position that would not be watched.

Now Ben grinned at them all.

'The only way in is down those cliffs. I hope you have a good head for heights, gentlemen. Once down, you'll be in Pepe's hands.'

'You'll be coming too?'

Ben shook his head. Jeff frowned.

'Not me. I've seen all I want to see of that camp at a distance. If you want to put your head in the vulture's nest, it's your business. All I want is a shot at that butcher who killed my pa!'

Jeff looked at Wang.

'You willing to have a go?'

Wang shrugged.

'What about the boy?'

Wang shook his head. 'He no climber! Boy slip, we

have no guide to camp.'

Jeff went to the edge of the jagged cliff and studied the sheer drop below. There were jagged rocks rearing up like twisted moss-grown teeth. A man would never survive a fall. Birds fluttered, wheeling and landing on rocks stained white with droppings.

He walked a few yards, considering, then came back to the waiting men.

'It can be done. There's ledges and handholds and the rock doesn't look crumbly. We could make a sling and Ben could help lower it bit by bit to the ground. What about it, Pepe? Another gold eagle if you'll climb down and take us to your hidey-holes.'

Pepe was looking white after taking a quick peep over the cliff but the lure of another gold eagle excited him. His eyes gleamed greedily.

'You'll give me two gold eagles?'

Jeff nodded. 'Is it a deal?'

'You bet! I'd even fly like the condors for two gold eagles!'

Jeff grinned. 'I'm not asking the impossible, Pepe. All I want you to do, is come down there with Wang and me so that we can reconnoitre what might become a battlefield. Right?'

Pepe nodded eagerly. They ate a frugal meal while using their ropes to make a sling. Then Ben tested the knots while Wang and Jeff stripped off their heavy jackets, checked guns and ammunition and finally announced they were ready to start.

Wang elected to climb down first, and only to use

the sling as a safety measure. He didn't trust just being lowered like a bundle of merchandise. He figured that if anything went wrong, at least he had his hands and feet to cling on to the rock with.

So Jeff and Ben cautiously paid out the strong rawhide ropes and patiently waited as Wang groped for and found handholds and lowered himself, inch by inch. The men watching could see the sheen of sweat breaking out on Wang, so that even the red sweatband around his head turned black.

Jeff gave a sigh of relief as Wang jumped clear and waved his arms, his thin inscrutable face breaking out in a beaming smile.

Then Jeff turned to a sweating Pepe, who rolled his eyes in fear as he was fastened in the sling. He clung convulsively at the ropes as Jeff pushed him to the edge of the cliff. The hundred-foot drop appeared deeper. His eyes grew misty as he backed off.

'Come on, Pepe! Think of those two gold eagles!'

Pepe gulped.

'I can't . . .' he began as vertigo enveloped him and he wanted to be sick. 'Mother of God, help me!'

Then without any more ado, Jeff pushed him over the edge. With a scream, Pepe swung out into space and then crashed against the wall, his flailing feet bouncing him from it.

Jeff grabbed the rope alongside Ben and held on, taking the strain from the rest of the rope which was bound around a jagged finger of rock.

Pepe was about twelve feet from the ground when the shot came. The bullet crashed into the cliff ridge at Jeff's feet. He felt its hot breath as it lifted a puff of dirt. Instinctively both men ducked; the rope skidded quickly and Pepe fell to the ground.

But Wang was already seeking out the gunman. He saw a flicker of movement and when the man's head rose again from behind a rock, Wang was already running and weaving towards him.

The astonished man's eyes widened as he saw how near he was but before he could gather his wits and fire, Wang's knife sailed through the air, blade over handle like a silver streak, and embedded itself in his chest.

The man gurgled and clawed at the quivering knife but it had penetrated too deeply. Blood gushed from his mouth and he disappeared behind the rocks.

Wang climbed to where the man had been hiding and turned the body over dispassionately. He yanked out his knife and wiped it on the man's shirt. He was truly dead, his staring eyes wide open. Wang ran through his pockets and found a few pesetas and a dirty rag. But he had a nearly full *bandolera* and he took that and his gun and knife. He hefted the gun and smiled. A very useful addition to his own arsenal.

It was only then that he went and examined Pepe, who'd crashed on to his shoulder and head and was now sitting up, dazed, and fingering a bump on his head with tender fingers.

'You all right, boy?'

Pepe nodded, still dazed.

Wang looked upwards and waved. Jeff and Ben had watched the little drama, never doubting the outcome.

'You ready to come down, Jeff?' Wang called. Jeff waved in return and began the climb down. He hesitated. He had to climb, for there was no way that Ben could hold the sling safely despite the rope being securely tied.

Wang held the rope firmly at the bottom and Jeff began the descent. He felt happier at having the rope at hand, at least he could grab it during the difficult parts and perhaps use it at resting points.

He was no climber like Wang and his respect for the little man grew, for Wang had made it look easy. But there were good hand- and footholds and when Jeff got into the rhythm of it, even though his muscles felt as if they'd been stretched to the limit, he began to make good time.

His foot slipped, loose chippings of rock fell away and, his heart thumping, he reached wildly for the rope. His body, already falling, was jerked to a swinging halt, his shoulder feeling as if it had been pulled out of its socket.

Then Ben's cry from above alerted him to a new danger. He risked a glance upwards and saw with horror that the rope coming from above was snagged on a jutting rock and was fraying fast, no doubt weakened already by the outlaw's bullet.

Convulsively, Jeff clawed at the rock. Now he was spreadeagled with arms outstretched, his feet digging into tiny cracks.

He felt the sweat burst from him in little rivulets. His bowels turned to water. Jesus Christ! The words screamed in his head, his teeth gritted, his eyes bulged. What a way to die! The thought was fleeting. Why the hell should he? Goddammit, he wasn't finished yet, his heart still beat and though he was spreadeagled like some limpet on a rock he had a chance. . . .

His head having cooled and his panic more under control, he took stock of the surrounding rock. He saw that to the right of him and a few feet down was a thin green sapling growing out of a crack. Maybe its roots went deep, looking for moisture.

He looked up at Ben who was watching anxiously.

'Can you snap that rope, Ben. I'll catch it and try to make for that tree. Once over there, I'll be fine.'

Ben caught on to what he meant to do and yanked several times at the rope. It parted and snaked down on to Jeff's shoulders. Clinging on with one hand, Jeff shoved the surplus over one shoulder and then negotiated the few feet with great care, finally grabbing the sapling at its base. He found it was whiplike and sappy.

He breathed a sigh of relief. His dread had been that the sapling might loosen from its precarious position and come out, roots and all.

He clung, aware of slipping feet as he wound the

end of the rope about the sapling and tugged. It appeared strong and to be holding but the crunch would come when he put his weight on it and swung down over a slight overhang.

He took a deep breath, waved to Wang watching from below and allowed himself to reach out and find another crevice lower down the cliff. He was now on his way.

The shadows had lengthened when he finally reached the bottom. He was winded and weak and he drank deeply from Wang's canteen. His limbs, unused to such exertion, trembled uncontrollably.

'I feel like shit,' he muttered to Wang. 'I don't know whether all this is worth it.'

Wang looked serious.

'Yes, but more to the point, Jeff, how do we get out now the rope is no more use to us? Unless of course he knows other ways.' They both looked at the sleeping Pepe who snored oblivious of the drama that had unfolded.

Six

El Condor and his men galloped hard up the winding trail. The man driving the four horses that pulled the army wagon was standing up, balancing on the shafts, a huge bullwhip cracking at the beasts' hindquarters. He yelled each time he wielded the whip to encourage them to more speed up the gruelling track. It was never meant for heavy wagons and there was danger that the wheels might come adrift at any time.

But Saigo was an experienced wagondriver. He'd taken over from Julio, having been on many treks across the plains before he took to ambushing lonely pilgrims and pillaging their wagons before setting them afire.

He'd been chased out of Texas and was now a refugee throwing in his lot with El Condor. He liked the danger and excitement of the headlong gallop, when a foot wrong could send horses and wagon over the cliff edge. To his own danger he never gave a thought. It was all in the hands of God.

El Condor's eyes searched the skyline as he rode. He knew as they all did that the next hour or two would be when they were most vulnerable. They were coming to the Devil's Gap, the scene of many ambushes in the past by the Indian Mescaleros. He also listened for that ghost trumpet. He was uneasy. The whole raid had gone too well. . . .

Suddenly there was a shout and looking behind him he saw that the wagon was all askew with one back wheel spinning wildly and overhanging the gorge below. The horses squealed and kicked, straining at the traces and gradually the weight of the wagon was dragging, taking the horses with it.

El Condor pulled up in a consuming rage. He'd wanted Saigo to bring the wagon up in the rear. Now there were only six men in front and the rest were holed up behind the wagon. Jesus, son of Mary, he raged, will the fool never learn?

Saigo was jumping free and tugging at one of the lead horses to help pull the horses forward. El Condor saw the horse rear and kick out at Saigo. The men available were in a mêlée of plunging horses as they tried to help stop the sliding wagon.

El Condor was more worried about the wagon than the men's safety. The wagon and its contents were the reason for the raid in the first place.

'Yoke more horses and drag that wagon back on track,' he bawled. 'Get those behind to shove. Goddammit! Use your brains if you have any! And you, Saigo, control those hosses and use that whip!'

'Why don't you get off that hoss and help?' Saigo yelled back angrily as he sidestepped another plunging hoof.

El Condor didn't answer, but he tucked away the challenging insolence in the back of his mind. Saigo's days were numbered. It had been a mistake allowing him into the outfit. He was just a madheaded son of a bitch whose fuse was ready to blow. . . .

Ben Jackson watched the little drama down below and when he saw that Jeff was OK, whistled softly and gestured to the far hills. Jeff reckoned he was going back to camp for reinforcements. Now they were on their own.

Ben could move faster on his own, his muscular legs eating up the miles, and he moved at a dogtrot, his eyes on the terrain and always figuring short cuts. His sense of direction was uncanny.

He walked into camp just as Lucia was ladling out stew for supper. He slumped down by the fire as if he'd no control over his legs. Without a word, she offered him the steaming jack-rabbit stew. He nodded in appreciation and started to eat ravenously while she doled out stew for the others before scraping the blackened pot for the remainder for herself.

Ely poured strong black stand-your-spoon-upright coffee in a mug and laced it well with brown sugar, then offered it mutely to Ben. All of them respected a man's hunger and need. He would give them the news as soon as he'd recovered.

They ate and waited until Ben was replete and belching satisfactorily. He stretched himself, feet to the fire, and told them of the sling fraying and how the three men were now down in the valley with no way of getting out except by climbing the crags, as the only entrance and exit was the narrow gap that led into the hills.

There was silence for a while as they all digested the news and considered the men's chances. Ely drew his corncob pipe and lighted up, emitting foul smoke which Lucia particularly detested, but it kept the night insects away. Ely spat juicy tobacco juice into the fire while he considered what had to be done.

He'd been a sergeant, campaigning all through the War between the States. Now his military mind was taking over.

'Any sign of El Condor in the camp?'

Ben shook his head.

'As far as we could see all was quiet. We saw a couple of look-outs near the gap, high up, and there was some toing and froing from the hovels they call homes. Pepe said the few men left behind to guard the camp, play hookey when the boss is gone and get high on hooch and argue over poker games. Pepe says sometimes there's gunplay and a killin'. That's when El Condor blows his top when he returns and he's judge, jury and executioner when that happens.

He does his own killin', just like he did at the Alamo . . .'

His voice tailed away and he poured more coffee and drank to hide the sudden surge of fury within him.

'Then we can reckon Jeff and Wang can look after themselves, but the kid will be the danger,' Ely ruminated. 'He could squawk.'

Ben disagreed.

'He's too scared of the cook. He knows what could happen to him if they catch him. Jeff and Wang will close-herd him. He knows all the ins and outs of that camp. He'll be useful.'

'How much ammo did they take with them?'

'All of it, even what I carried. Jeff was also carrying some sticks of dynamite.'

'Mmm, it might be an idea to get to hell over there and plug that gap. What d'you say, fellers?' Ely grinned with delight. This was like old times.

Ben looked uncertain; his mind was more on seeking out El Condor and putting a bullet into the place that would do most good. He wasn't for joining in an all-out war.

Tijuana sat up, eyes gleaming, his hands flexing as he thought of the blowing-up of the only opening into the valley and the prospect of knocking off the men like sitting ducks down below in the narrow gorge. An exhilarating way to do some target practice!

Tijuana's answer was to pull out his six-guns, take

100

them apart and clean and polish them. He handled them lovingly as if they were his best friends.

'When do we start?' was his only comment.

'Tomorrow, as soon as we get organized,' answered Ely.

'What about her?' Red Baines asked, pointing with his thumb.

'She stays in camp,' Ely snapped. 'What else?'

Lucia looked from one to the other. Ben was now asleep.

'Stop talking about me as if I'm some doll! I have a say in this and I'm *not*, I say *not* staying here by myself! I'm coming with you!'

Ely gave a bark of laughter.

'Lady, you're talkin' out of yore backside! Are you loco or somethin'? We're not on a Sunday picnic. We're goin' to force-march across and over those hills and we're gonna have ourselves just a teensy-weensy bit of a fight at the end of it. Now would a lady want to get mixed up in that?'

'I'm no lady!'

Tijuana sat up then, eyes wickedly gleaming.

'Yeah? Well what about a bit of . . .'

She reached over and slapped his face.

'There's ladies and respectable females. I'm one of them and don't you forget it!' Then she turned fiercely to Ely. 'Don't you forget I know as much about that camp as Pepe does and as Pepe isn't here with you, maybe I could be useful.'

Ely contemplated her grimly.

'You're a mighty fine respectable female, but I can't see you trekkin' over them there hills. It'll be ride some and walk some. How about that?'

'I'll manage. You won't hear me complain. Besides, I can shoot. I'd be another hand.'

'It'll mean packin' up camp and usin' the nags as pack-horses. We'll leave what we don't need. Just take essentials and trust to luck. Mind you, we'll not stop if you crack along the way. You'd have to fend for youself!'

She quailed inside at his threat but faced him firmly. She'd be damned if she'd weaken. She'd show the sons of bitches!

'I'll not crack!'

He nodded. 'Right. You ride with us tomorrow. Now get some sleep.'

Jeff dragged Pepe up to his feet and shook him.

'Come on, Pepe, this is no time to sleep!'

Pepe opened his eyes wide, his hand going to his head.

'What ... where am I?' He looked about him, dazed.

'You're back where you came from, Pepe. Now come on, look lively and show us some of the secret places you know of.'

Wang, who'd been inspecting the dead body of the outlaw, now came bounding back to them.

'Him concussed?'

'Yeah, a bit but he's coming round. Hell, he'd better.' Jeff shoved his hip-flask into Pepe's mouth. 'Drink you son of a bitch.' He tipped Pepe's head back until he choked. 'Don't waste it, drink it!'

Pepe gulped, shook his head and pushed Jeff away. 'I'm awake. I'm fine.'

'Then let's get moving. You lead the way, Pepe. We want to find a place to hole up, then tonight we go out and do a fast check. Right?'

Pepe nodded, then, taking a quick look around, started off at a dogtrot. Jeff and Wang, hefting their gear, followed more warily, on the watch for any more alert guards. There was none and they travelled fast down the valley, dodging behind boulders and taking advantage of every hillock and bush.

Pepe, grinning, brought them to a vantage point and, looking around with pride, said softly, 'There you are, number one hideout.'

Jeff and Wang looked about them and even sharp-eyed Wang was nonplussed.

'What the hell are you talking about? Where's the hideout?' said Wang, looking out at the surrounding scenery: hills on one side and a steep incline down to the camp itself on the other.

Then Pepe pointed at an old gnarled tree, long dead. It clung, dead roots still entwined, to the rock. Many of its branches were partly split and leaning over to the ground amidst a pile of smaller dead branches. Even the birds found them useless.

Jeff stared at it, then went closer to examine it

further and saw the small aperture leading into the tangled mess. Cautiously he bent and crawled inside and was amazed, for there at the foot of the tree was a hole in the ground. Perhaps the tree had died long years ago because of that hole.

It smelled of mountain cat and the foetid stench of rotted meat. He felt rather than saw the bones of dead animals. He crawled out.

'How long since this was an animal's den?'

Pepe shrugged. 'I been comin' to this here hole for two . . . three years and never saw no animal, not even a fox. It be a nigh-dead place. It be big inside. Take all us and more, it will.'

'How did you find it?'

'Climbed up a ways, lookin' for a way out. A goat path goes so far but not to the top. It be a good place to hide kinda quick like.'

Jeff nodded. 'We'll eat and then take a look-see and figure how many are still here.'

'I can tell you that, *señor*. The cook, God rot him, and not more than ten others.'

'Counting those at the entrance?'

Pepe nodded vigorously.

'That's how it's always been.'

'So shouldn't be any different now.' Jeff smiled at Wang. 'Maybe we should give 'em a surprise before the rest of the outfit arrives!'

Wang grinned. 'Now you're talkin'. Just like the old days!'

'No need to waste time laying up for tonight. We

should be able to get close and lob a couple of sticks of "old smokey".'

Pepe looked at one and then the other, not comprehending.

'Old smokey? What's that?'

'Dynamite. We take 'em out with dynamite.'

Pepe's eyes bulged, then he grinned.

'Serve 'em right, especially that son of a bitch cook. I hope he rots in hell!'

They left the gear they didn't need: the heavy ropes, the canteens and the food they'd brought, and loaded up with ammunition, Jeff carrying the precious sticks of dynamite.

Wang scouted ahead, taking advantage of scrub and rocks, Jeff moving lightly behind him and Pepe stumbling along. Several times Jeff had to remind the youth to move quietly. Jeese! He was more a hindrance than a help.

They scouted the perimeter of the camp and found the hovels empty and smelling foul. Faint laughter came from a larger hut and Jeff reckoned Pepe was right: the men were having themselves a drinking session while the boss was away.

So they were all together. There would never be a better chance to wipe them all out at the same time.

They paused, listening. A last look round, then they began to run across the open space in front of the hut. Jeff and Wang parted company in military fashion, then Wang ran behind the hut, ready to dispatch anyone trying to escape, and Jeff went to the front, with Pepe at his back.

He pulled out the two cigar-shaped sticks and, waving Pepe back, crouched low. Shielding his tinderbox against any wind, he struck a lucifer. The wind caught the flame and it blew out, Jeff cursed.

He was fumbling for another lucifer when the door opened and a man came out, laughing and unbuttoning his flies. They stared at each other in shock, then the outlaw opened his mouth to yell. But Jeff's knife took him in the chest. As he fell forward Jeff wound his fingers into his shirt and lifted and dragged the man half-way clear.

'Hey there, Paco, shut that damned door! You're lettin' the goddamn wind in!' came the shout.

Jeff motioned to Pepe and mouthed, help me you idiot! Pepe sprang forward, his eyes big as he watched the man who'd bullied him for years, then, pulling with all their might, they dumped the body around the corner of the hut.

But it was too late. A giant of a man was standing in the doorway, and Jeff had dropped the dynamite when confronted with Paco. The newcomer stared at it, then he gave a great yell which brought the other men tumbling out of the hut while the giant was fanning out a fusillade of warning shots.

Pepe panicked and started to run but ran the wrong way and took a bullet in the chest. He spun around, a scream dying on his lips. Jeff was aware of the boy's mistake but took advantage of it, to roll behind a water butt. He took the big man in the throat.

The shots kicked up dirt and at first it was easy to fire into the bunch struggling to get out of the doorway. It was like potting rats at bay in a corner.

Then as a couple or three bodies fell across the doorway, the others took refuge inside and Jeff was uncomfortbly aware that someone was shooting from the small window. He felt the hum of a bullet skim his cheek. He felt the sticky hot blood drip on to his shirt-front.

Then, without warning, there was a carrump and a blast of smoke and flame. He flung himself flat on the ground as it rained wood spars, bits of furniture, and slithers of bloodied flesh. . . .

He smiled. Good old Wang. At least he'd used his brains and lit the spare stick of dynamite, even though he, Jeff, might have been killed.

A bloody-faced man crawled to what was left of the doorway. Jeff got him in his sights and put him out of misery.

Shakily, he got to his feet and searched for the sticks of dynamite. They would be needed, no doubt, as a welcome home for El Condor.

El Condor was in a rage.For all the efforts of the men and the extra horses, the wagon would not budge. The weight had increased at the back as the heavy load slipped and the trapped wheel had ground loose some of the rock which had hurtled down below. It looked as if the whole damned wagon was going to be lost.

'Saigo, you get up there and throw out the money-chest and the guns and as much of the food sacks as you can. Now get to it!'

Saigo stared at him.

'You must be joking, *Coronel!* Any movement on the wagon and it could be gone in seconds!'

They stared each other out as the men at the innerside of the blocked wagon watched the clash of two strong-willed men. All were in favour of Saigo handling the task. He was the one fool enough to ride like the devil up the narrow winding trail. It was he who'd gambled and lost. He should now gamble his own life again.

'Saigo. I command here. If you don't obey I shall consider it mutiny.'

'So?' Saigo's grin was mocking. 'What will you do? You need men like me amongst these sheep.' He looked at the other men contemptuously. 'Let one of them do the donkey work.'

'I said you, Saigo. Up there, now. We are wasting time.'

Suddenly El Condor's rifle was pointing at Saigo's middle. Saigo laughed recklessly and then shrugged and climbed warily on to the tilting wagon.

He stood with legs apart, balancing as the wagon shuddered and then settled again. The men watching let out their breath as the wagon creaked and subsided. Saigo moved forward gingerly, picked up a sack of flour and threw it overboard. Nothing happened and he reached for another.

El Condor moved impatiently.

'Leave the sacks and concentrate on the guns and get that chest out!'

Saigo spoke viciously.

'If you want them so badly, come up here and help me. The sacks are on top of the guns and chest and I'm no miracle worker!' He threw out another sack, this time of coffee which burst on the ground, the beans spreading into the dirt. The men groaned. How long had it been since they'd drunk real coffee?

Saigo grew bolder. He moved a couple of sacks of chilli beans and tried to drag out a long wooden case containing rifles. It was solidly weighted down and though Saigo was a big man, his own vast strength would not shift it.

'God blast it to hell!' he called. 'It'll take all day to shift this lot. Get one of them sons of bitches up here to help me!'

El Condor surveyed the inside of the wagon. Saigo was telling the truth. The wagon's load had shifted dangerously into a heap.

He thought of all his plans to acquire the army's cash and guns. The supplies had been a bonus. He cursed luridly.

He motioned to one of the staring Mexicans, a useless piece of cannon fodder, he reckoned, who wouldn't be missed if he plunged down into the gorge.

'You there, get aboard and help Saigo!'

The man blanched but reluctantly climbed clumsily aboard. El Condor noted in passing that the peon's pants were wet. Saigo looked at the puny man with disgust. How much help would he be?

'Come on now, *amigo*. Use those puny muscles and help me lift!'

The peon took a deep breath and he and Saigo began to drag the gun-chest clear. Under it could be seen the money-chest tantalizingly close yet unmovable. The peon shifted nervously and the wagon groaned and teetered, sending the horses in the traces into a frenzy.

There were screams and yells from men who tried to save the horses. Knives slashed at leather thongs as the wagon slipped and harness stretched tight. Then, as the lead horses broke free, the weight of the wagon dragged the rest with it over the edge and Saigo and the peon were catapulted into the air. With limbs flailing, they screamed their way down into the gorge below.

El Condor stood paralysed, staring into the depths, oblivious of the hubbub going on around him as the men tried to quieten the remainder of the animals.

He couldn't believe it was possible. All he'd planned for to be lost because of a stupid, arrogant cretin who laughed at danger. Who in his right mind would have whipped those horses to a frenzy until they took that narrow hill trail which wound so near the edge of the gorge? Only a fool or a madman would do such a thing. He ground his teeth in frustration. The cash he so much needed, the guns and ammunition and the supplies, all gone for ever.

The rest of the outfit were crowding the narrow trail now that the wagon was gone. He looked them all over. They were all waiting for his reaction and his command.

'Well? What are you staring at? Let's move on.'

'But the supplies? We need . . .' one of the men called.

'What of them? They're gone. Finished!' He mounted his horse and without looking back moved up the trail.

The men followed more slowly, grumbling amongst themselves. Instead of real coffee, it would be acorn mush again, and bread with weevils in it. It wasn't good enough for men who'd been promised the best of everything if they followed El Condor.

Ben Jackson was a slave-driver, at least Lucia thought so. She ached in every limb and was so tired her eyes drooped as she walked. Her feet were blistered and each step was agony, yet she held her head high. She wouldn't give in and even repulsed Tijuana when he offered her his arm.

But when they rested she was past helping to cook the meal. If there was a spring, she sat bathing her feet. If not, she lay on her blanket and took her share of the disgusting home brew that Ben brought forth at these times. She would shudder at the hot raw taste but it put new life into her.

There was not much conversation, except perhaps between Ben and Ely. The rest of them put their trust in the trumpet man. He knew the terrain and by the way he was pushing them, they would be soon at the camp.

Now he spoke to them all.

'Eat well now, for our next push will be the last and God knows when we'll eat again. We're all tired and worn out, so you folk eat and sleep. I'll keep watch.'

Lucia, relieved that the nightmare force-marching was nearly over, and frightened at what was to come, found it hard to eat. All she wanted was to curl up in her blanket and sleep. But Ben's keen eyes were upon her.

'You eat, d'you hear, or else we'll be leavin' you behind and you don't want that, do you?'

'Not after coming all this far in these conditions,' she said tiredly and forced down her share of last night's cold stewed beef and stale bread. The hot coffee helped but she didn't even remember putting down the coffee-mug, she was fast asleep.

Tijuana tucked the blanket around her and stared accusingly at Ben.

'Did we have to travel so fast? We've nearly killed her.'

Ben shrugged. 'She knew the score. It's vital we get back to the camp before El Condor. Remember Jeff and Wang and the boy are down in that camp. They need our help.'

112

Red Baines stirred, opening one eye after pulling his hat from his face.

'He's right, Tijuana. We can't put a woman's needs before the lives of others.'

All too soon, Ben was shaking their shoulders. Blinking they came awake, Lucia with a groan and the feeling she'd just dropped off to sleep. Dowsing her face in cold mountain water soon brought her sharply alive again. The rest of the men grumbled amongst themselves.

After two hours of walking and dragging reluctant horses not used to carrying heavy loads over rough ground, they paused at last while Ben went forward and scanned the land beyond the ridge. They were back overlooking the camp and the early morning sun sent a clear light over all, accentuating the open patches of ground and making deep shadows in the clefts of land and the sparse clustering of trees.

Ben's eyes grew wide with surprise when he saw the devastation in the midst of the camp; a great rounded patch of blackened, still-smouldering rubble which spread far beyond the camp in a soot-blackened ring that resembled a star blaze. It looked damn well like the remains of an explosion to Ben. He turned and waved to Ely and Red to come up and take a look.

Ely laughed. 'It looks mighty like Jeff and the boys don't need us! He sure hasn't lost his touch! Any sign of 'em?'

Ben slowly swivelled the field-glasses in all directions. Then he shook his head.

'All's quiet. You think we should go on down?'

'That was the plan, but turn them there glasses on yon gap first. No need to hurry. We could be walkin' into a trap.'

Ben took his time and then gave a little shout.

'There's Wang perched high and he's wavin' to us and grinnin' like crazy! It's the all-clear. He began to hunt for an easy way down.

'Hold your hosses! What about her and the others?' Red roared, gesturing to Lucia and the waiting men. 'This takes thinkin' out.' Red looked at Ely for confirmation.

Ely nodded. 'No need for everyone to climb down into the valley. Besides, we have the horses to deal with. Look, I'll go down there and see what Jeff has cookin'. You, Ben, will cut trail and lead Red and the others further down the pass and Lucia can look after the horses while you fellers find a good place to hide out on each side of the trail. It's got to be within signalling distance from us at the head of the pass. Right? We gotta have those bastards boxed in.'

Red Baines grinned and spat.

'Just like old times when we boxed in those Yanks at Cotton Hill.'

'You got the idea, Red. Now get movin'.'

Ely waited only long enough to drink from his canteen and hitch up his supplies, then he was ready to tackle the steep incline.

He had the advantage over the others. He need

114

not watch out for enemy bullets, but he hesitated; it was a long way down if he missed his footing. Jesus! He was getting too old for this lark, but he would never have admitted this to Jeff.

Gritting his teeth and averting his eyes from what was far below he began the steep descent. He found it easier than he'd expected, for there were tufts of coarse grass and brushwood that he could grab. Loose rocks, disturbed, rocketed downwards, but that part of the valley was far more undulating than further up where the valley entered a steep gorge.

Sliding and stumbling he made his way down, a sheen of sweat beading his brow and the back of his neck. His leg muscles felt stiff and tense and it was with huge relief he saw that he was but a few feet from the bottom. He jumped and rolled and hit the ground hard, knocking the breath out of himself. He lay winded, his heart pumping until his blood ceased to pound in his ears.

Then he was up and taking his bearings. The remains of the camp were on his left, the gap out of the valley on the right. He set off at a easy jog-trot. The sooner he contacted the others, the better.

A sharp whistle had him searching the skyline and he saw Wang perched on a rock. He was waving his arms and grinning.

Then he was coming down the escarpment like a lean and hungry puma. He clapped Ely on the back in unaccustomed welcome.

'You made it, Ely. I hope you brought some grub

with you. We're all tuckered out.'

Ely grinned. 'What the hell d'you think I'm totin'? A load of rocks? Where's Jeff and the Mex and the boy?'

'The boy didn't make it. Panicked and walked into a slug,' Wang said without emotion. 'The boss and that greasy Mex are plantin' the last of the dynamite. We got the whole goddam trail wired up. I gotta go back up there and watch out. Those bastards could come along at any time.'

'Here, take this with you.' Ely fumbled in his bag and brought out bread and cold beef. Wang took it hungrily. 'Where's the boss now?'

'Up there.' Wang waved to a massive overhang. 'If that lot comes down like he figures, it'll fill the whole trail.'

'I'd better go look him up.' But there was no need. He saw Jeff paying out a rope and went to help hold it steady while Wang climbed back to his outpost, eating as he went.

Jeff climbed down and Tijuana followed. Ely brought them up to date on what was happening above.

'So Red will be able to signal to us when El Condor's bunch get into the pass?'

'Yeah, you'll be able to calculate just when to blow the trail.'

'Good. I figured that Red would catch on. Now all we can do is get to our posts and wait. We'll eat and Tijuana will take the other side while we stay on this.

Tijuana knows to wait for my signal.'

Tijuana nodded. 'I got it off pat, boss. The whole damn world will blow up when you give the signal.' He grinned. 'I can't wait!'

Down the valley, hovering over the burned-out camp, the vultures were already gathering. Far above them, twisting and turning silently on the updraughts, was a condor, watching, waiting.

Seven

El Condor was aware of the grumbles behind him as he rode on. He would ignore the situation for the moment, but he wouldn't forget those who mouthed off the loudest. There was the right time and the wrong time to discipline the troops. At this time, he needed the goodwill of most of his men. But the time would come. . . .

He reined in, holding up his hand, and the weary men pulled up thankfully. It had been a long haul crossing the river into Texas and then travelling with fires up their backsides back into Mexico with only the good God knowing what size posse was after them. The military might of northern America had long arms, and the subsequent loss had knocked the stuffing out of them.

They were a dejected group who camped rough on the narrow trail that night. There was no celebratory singing, of a job well done. They ate hard tack, drank brackish water from their canteens, rolled into their blankets and slept.

It was all too soon morning. The men stretched, aware of night-time sweat, dry throats and the dark cloud of failure lying heavily on them. All they wanted was to get back to camp and forget this fiasco. They were all shaken, for this was the first time El Condor's plans had failed.

Of course it wasn't his fault, someone reasoned. But it had been El Condor's fault. Someone had to be responsible and he was the boss man. He should have dispatched Saigo at once. He should have known that Saigo was no good. He'd always been an arrogant bastard and unpopular. El Condor should have shot him on day one.

So they grumbled to themselves and El Condor maintained a stiff silence, holding himself remote from what was going on, but very much aware. . . .

They moved on. It would be the last leg before reaching camp. The horses too seemed to know instinctively that they were on home territory. There would be food and rest for them and a scrubby green pasture to run in.

El Condor quickened his pace and the men following broke into a gentle gallop. Soon this nightmare sortie would be over. All eyes were looking ahead now, for the signal from the two look-out men positioned on each side of the gap.

They were coming up hard and fast to the gap in the hills and now El Condor was frowning. Why had the two men not been there waving their hats and giving the usual all clear?

The thought had no sooner sliced through his mind than it seemed as if the whole world blew up.

El Condor's horse screamed and reared wildly, while those behind him squealed and plunged. A great blast of heat and wind tore down on them, lifting men and horses high as rocks and debris rained down on them.

El Condor was thrown from his horse as it collapsed with a broken leg. It kicked hard, and El Condor rolled away shielding his head with his arms as hard-baked clay and boulders and even scrub-brush pounded down from the skies.

Then came another explosion, this time sending rubble over a wider area. Now he saw that not only was the gap obliterated, but much of the trail had been buried and along with it men and horses.

He dragged himself to a jumble of rocks and squeezed himself into a hole big enough for a dog. He waited for another onslaught. Some *bastardo* up there was using dynamite. He recognized dynamite. He'd used it himself on occasion. He reckoned it must be the military. But how the hell had they gotten themselves here so quickly and how did they know the location of the camp?

He lay quiet, waiting, but as no more explosions came he grew bold and crawled out of the hole. It was then he saw the real devastation.

There were dead horses and horses that lay kicking in agony, their squeals a cacophony of sound mingling with the groans of men bloodied and confused.

There were those who lay sprawled in death and those who were even now trying to stand up, swaying dazedly.

A rifle bullet screamed and a man's chest erupted into a mass of red. He was flung back hard and hit the ground. El Condor bellowed a warning, and an instinct to survive made those capable of moving quickly roll behind dead horses or behind boulders.

Helplessly, El Condor watched. He had lost his rifle when his horse collapsed. He needed another and he must crawl at least a hundred yards to get the one dropped by one of his men.

The rifle fire was intermittent. It surprised El Condor as he expected a full blown troop at the very least. Where were they all? Why were they playing cat and mouse?

Then, raking the skyline, El Condor had the answer. There were no soldiers. He saw the tell-tale puffs of smoke after the rifle fire. He and his men were being held down by what must be a small posse of men, no doubt led by some smartarse sheriff!

He took a chance, and crouching ran along the line of men. Those riding at the back had come off best. They were now quieting frightened horses and though some were suffering from flying objects he could see that at least half of his men were recovering from the initial shock. He waved his arms.

'Back! Get back! The gap's closed! We must find another way to get out!'

He grabbed the reins of a riderless horse and leapt

aboard. It plunged and reared but he gripped it firmly with both legs, yanking cruelly at the bit.

Some of the men looked at him uncomprehendingly. He cursed.

'God dammit! Are you all deaf?'

Suddenly the rifle fire came again and this time the men with him realized they were indeed under attack. One man screamed and somersaulted out of his saddle. El Condor was just in time to see where the fire was coming from.

He fired twice but the rifle was old and not well cared for. He cursed the owner's carelessness and for the first time El Condor felt the rising panic within him. Were they all going to be shot down at leisure by a bunch of ill-trained deputies, like some small-time owlhooters? Not if he had anything to do with it!

It was time to take action. He quelled the rising terror. After all, he was the famous or infamous Coronel Fernandez, the scourge of the Mexican Army, depending on the point of view of *compadres* or victims.

'Get under cover,' he shouted, and keep your eyes peeled. There's only a handful of the bastards. We'll get 'em and then we'll ride down the trail and into the foothills.'

'What about the camp?' someone bawled.

'Forget the camp,' he snapped. 'Whoever threw that dynamite wouldn't leave the camp intact. It's gone! We're finished up there.'

There came no answer to that for the rifle fire came again and this time it seemed that there were reinforcements. Perhaps he had been wrong and someone *was* up there playing a game of cat and mouse.

El Condor gritted his teeth. It was like trying to fight ghosts. There had been no sightings of men, just the devastating rifle fire from men who knew how to shoot.

Then chillingly, El Condor heard the faint strains of a trumpet as it sounded the call to arms. Sweat poured from him and his hands shook.

Someone out there was taunting him, bringing back flashes of those last days before the fall of the Alamo. El Condor felt the shadow of doom hanging over him.

Suddenly he lost control. Swiftly turning his horse to face the barren ridge of rock rising high above his head he shook his fist and screamed, 'Come on and show your face! Get it over with! If you want me, come and get me!'

The men watched, appalled. They had seen El Condor in murderous rages and watched him shoot a man just because he didn't like the look in the victim's eye but this was something new. It was the reaction of a frightened man and El Condor's stature was shrinking fast.

They all heard the trumpet call. The sound echoed across the peaks like the wail of a lost soul. The notes quivered, then stopped abruptly and the listeners' ears ached as they waited for the sound to come again. It was as if all the land and the birds were waiting.

Then, as the men relaxed, the sound came again, mocking and threatening.

One of the men was galvanized to action. He kicked his horse's ribs and it reared and plunged, then went at a mad gallop down the trail up which they had so recently come. Then panic was transferred to the others and soon there was a headlong gallop. El Condor watched, dazed for a while, then he followed more slowly.

Then came two explosions and the galloping men were screaming and swerving as tons of rock blew up into the air and came down with relentless precision, obliterating what had once been a long line of galloping men and horses.

Far above, Red, who'd watched the strung-out cavalcade of riders coming hell-bent, rubbed his hands with glee. He'd not lost his touch with dynamite. He knew he was still one of the best. He had the right feel for the stuff. He loved it.

He was also impressed with Ben, who'd been acting strange. He'd wandered off, muttering about giving 'em the usual rallying call. The son of a bitch certainly knew how to spook the bastards. They'd reacted mighty fast to the eerie call, no doubt about it; the mountains echoed the menace, not good for men under attack.

The woman crouched silently by Red, still shaking

from the ear-shattering blasts. Red had to give her credit. She'd not complained on the forced march and actually had come in useful by watching the horses when he and Ben had crawled away to plant the dynamite.

He watched Ben crawling back from his high lookout. He was grinning like a maniac.

'Did you see the bastards, how they panicked when they heard the trumpet?'

'Aye, lad, you sure scared the shit out of them, especially that son of a bitch, El Condor! Now why is he spooked by the sound of a trumpet?'

Ben scowled.

'It goes back a long time. You remember the Alamo?'

Red nodded. He spat.

'Aye, I remember some talk of it. The Texans forted up and held out for days. It was hunger and thirst that beat them, and the worry about the women and children.'

'That swine down there known as El Condor was General Santa Anna's hound-dog. He was the one who saw to it that Santa Anna's infamous orders were carried out, and he enjoyed the doing of it!'

'So that's it. The trumpet reminds him . . .'

'My pa was a sergeant in the fort. I was a lad of sixteen and the bugler. My pa made me hide when the outer walls of the fort were breached. I heard the screams of the few that were left. They even killed the wounded in the makeshift hospital. Only the women and children were left alive.' His voice broke. 'I heard my pa's death shriek. . . .'

Red put a hand on his shoulder.

'You've had a hard road to travel, but now it looks as if you're comin' to the end of it.'

They peered down into the smoke, which was now drifting upwards, and saw the utter devastation the explosion had caused.

There were still men alive down there and horses kicking. It was easy to aim slow and deliberate before shooting. It was like potting rats in a barn at harvest time.

At a touch on the shoulder Red turned sharply, rifle upraised. He lowered it hurriedly as he saw Jeff and Wang beside him.

'By God, you shouldn't creep up on a feller, ' he rasped, his throat dry and croaky from the smoke. Jeff grinned.

'I see you did a good job. You've not lost your touch!'

Red grinned in reply.

'Easiest job I ever did. No sweat, and I do believe we've nailed all the sons of bitches.'

Jeff nodded to Ben.

'I heard your trumpet, feller. Near on sent m'blood cold, it did. It sure took the heart out of that lot. Any sign of life down there?'

Red shrugged.

'We had us a shootin' contest. I think we got 'em all, but mebbe we should go down and make sure.

What about it?'

Then he looked at Wang who was busy cleaning his rifle and loading up again.

'Where's the youngster?'

'Pepe? Oh, he got his early on. Stuck his fool head up and got it blown off. Pity. He helped us find our way around the camp. I suppose we'll have to tell the woman.'

Lucia listened quietly while Jeff gave her a brief report on how Pepe died bravely. She sighed.

'He wouldn't be dead now if I hadn't begged him to take me out of that camp, but I should have gone mad if I'd had to stay longer.'

'Don't blame yourself, ma'am,' Jeff said gruffly. 'If he hadn't got out, he would most likely have been killed along with the others in camp, and yourself as well. So forget it.'

Then Jeff looked at the others.

'Well, it looks as if we should go down there and check 'em all out. We've gotta find El Condor's body. If we don't check, then we'll never know whether he got away.'

Ben nodded eagerly.

'I'll go. I'll even go alone if I have to.'

'No, we'll all go. The woman can stay with the horses.' With that, they began the long haul down the steep incline. It was dangerous work as now so much of the bedrock had been cracked and lifted and much of the top stratum of rock was loose.

They had to move cautiously as a careless step sent

rocks the size of a man's head tumbling down into the gorge and each rock dislodged others until became a small avalanche.

At last, breathing heavily and with aching legs, they reached the half-covered bodies of men and horses, now stiffening in death and even now covered with flies attracted by the stench of drying blood.

There were no survivors. Some had died as boulders showered down. Others lay where they'd been shot. A horse whinnied faintly under a mound of rubble. Jeff shot it in the head and then all was quiet.

Above, swooping and wheeling, their beady eyes assessing the carcasses, were several vultures attracted by the strong smell of carrion. A lone condor perched on a high peak before spreading wings that spanned ten feet, plunged down to take a look and then soared upwards, making use of a thermal draught of air.

Jeff Onslow looked after it, admiring its grace and beauty.

'There you go, old feller, king of the mountains! Even the eagles pay homage!'

His reverie was interrupted by a shout from Ben. He was pointing upwards on the other side of the gorge. Jeff's eyes followed and he saw the tiny figure of a man clawing his way upwards.

As he watched, the man half turned and a handgun spat, the bullet whining past Jeff who ducked instinctively. He heard a gasping shout and turned to

128

find Wang on his knees, his chest spouting blood. Jeff cursed and sprang to Wang's aid but he knew that it was too late.

It was his, Jeff's fault. He had been too sure that they were all safe. His eyes met Ben's.

'Look to Wang,' Jeff said grimly. 'I'm going up there after him.'

'No. Wang's your buddy. You see to him. That's El Condor up there and I'm gonna see that the business between us is finished once and for all!'

Jeff could do nothing but nod. He watched Ben scramble over the piles of rocks and boulders and start the hazardous climb up the steep, nearly perpendicular wall. The man climbing above moved slowly. Small rocks came tumbling down and Ben started his climb at one side to dodge the rocks. He shifted his trumpet to his back and threw away his rifle. At his side, he carried his Colt and at his back, the sheath-knife was snugly in place.

He was younger than El Condor and had the stamina of a man used to climbing the hills. He knew his legs would not give out. He would get the bastard if he had to die alongside him.

He'd waited a whole lifetime to catch up with Coronel Fernandez, the man who'd watched and participated in the massacre of the survivors of the Alamo . . .

He wouldn't fail now.

Eight

El Condor clung to the sheer wall of rock, lungs heaving, muscles stretched to breaking-point. His breath came in sobbing gasps. He had clawed his way up for nearly a hundred feet; the way above seemed endless and already the air was thinning.

The urge to look back and down overcame him. He had to look once more on the carnage below, and to see the enemy that had annihilated his men.

He saw the small bunch of men climbing down to investigate what was left of men and horses. Army scouts, sent down to give the all-clear, no doubt. His eyes raked the gorge but there was no sign of soldiers. Could it possibly be that this handful of men were all it took to wipe his men and his camp from the face of the earth?

The answer was as bitter gall in his mouth. He shook with anger and part of it was for himself. He'd grown arrogant and careless and had forgotten the first military law, to be aware at all times.

130

The thoughts had gone fleetingly through him. A moment in time. He saw one of the men look upwards and point and instinctively, expecting a rifle bullet, he pulled his Colt from its holster with great danger to himself. He fired a warning shot to deter them and give him little more time.

He saw with astonishment that the wild shot had indeed found a target. He saw one man drop and with a wild surge of strength and glee, he lunged for the next handhold and began to climb with renewed vigour.

At first, the granite rock provided good hand- and footholds. Fissures and crevices abounded. In some places there were signs of ancient water seepage, as if sand had long been washed away and only the rock remained. As he climbed higher he found birds had nested in the fissures.

Birds wheeled around him, disturbed and angry and he nearly lost his precarious handholds when a furious bird flew at him from her nest. He reached in and found a warm egg. Good, he thought exultantly, a raw egg would put new life into him.

He cracked it and found inside a half-formed chick. He threw it away disgustedly and climbed on.

It was gradually becoming plain that climbing this wild escarpment had not been a good idea. Where did it lead? At the peak would he find a way over the mountains and would there be water?

He paused yet again, to look up and consider. At this height he could see the top of the gorge but beyond that were other peaks and they were covered in snow. Dear God, would the top of the gorge lead to civilization or was he lost on what was called the skyline?

He took a quick look downwards, something he hadn't bothered to do before because of fear of vertigo. He was startled to see a lone pin-point of movement, a black spider that moved slowly upwards.

His heart pounded. He, Luis Fernandez, was a fugitive for the first time in his life! His body exuded the fear of the hunted.

He crouched on a narrow ledge and, twisting his body, sent off three wild downward shots from his Colt. He was dimly aware of the bullets ricocheting from the wall around the man in puffs of dust.

The man clung to the wall and El Condor took careful aim and shot again. This time on an empty cylinder. He cursed with rage and flung the Colt down towards the climbing man. Then in a frenzy of panic and despair, El Condor began to climb like a madman.

Down below, Ben Jackson clung to the mighty wall, the bullets whining before exploding against the wall beside him. Splinters of rock sprayed him with needles that jabbed him mercilessly, drawing blood on face and hands. Nothing lethal but uncomfortable and one splinter in his hand was causing blood to flow copiously which was dangerous for it made his hand slippery.

He gripped the rock with his good hand and unloosed his kerchief; clumsily he wrapped it around his cut hand. It might serve until the blood clotted. It would do so in this cold thinning temperature. He climbed doggedly on but now he took more care.

He was aware of the man above's frequent rest stops. The bastard was weakening. Ben exulted.

Ben, climbing more to the left of El Condor, found what could be called an aperture and rested for a spell, taking the time to look to his wounds and wipe the blood away. He drank from a canteen he was carrying on his back. He would amuse himself by playing his trumpet. . . .

The eerie sound wafted upwards. Ben himself was not to be seen because of the slight overhang. Shaken, El Condor nearly lost his grip on his next handhold as the notes sent out their order to advance.

Mother of God! That trumpet again! Was it real or was it in his head? Was he going loco for want of oxygen? El Condor looked down but the climber appeared to be gone. Had he fallen to his death and he, El Condor, been too preoccupied with his own survival to notice, or had the climber been a figment of his imagination?

The trumpet sounded again and this time the wailing notes of the last post came loud and clear and with them a message. He shuddered. Were all his ghosts coming back to haunt him?

Luis Fernandez remembered all the myths and legends he'd learned at his grandmother's knee in the days long before he became a soldier, but was just a small ignorant boy growing up amidst a wealth of superstition.

Suddenly he was heaving himself up from the wall to the flatter surface at the top of the gorge. He looked about him and down at the great gash in the ground that was the gorge and he exulted. He had made it and to hell with the ghosts!

He yelled the old battle cry that had so paralysed the enemy in days gone by. He shook both fists in the air, crying, 'You might kill my men but you can't destroy El Condor!'

Then he turned and surveyed the land in front of him. It was a desert of rock as far as he could see, both to the left and to the right. Nothing stirred, not even a bush to move in the cutting wind. It was a lifeless landscape. Before him were the foothills to even higher peaks.

Above him, wheeling silently in the thin air, was the condor, its giant shadow completely covering him. He imagined its beady eyes on him, assessing him as some succulent piece of carrion. . . .

Below, Ben Jackson, doggedly clinging to the rock face, climbed steadily, a great fury raging in him as all the old nightmares he'd ever suffered attacked him anew.

134

He heard himself playing his trumpet desperately, defiantly, as the last bombardment of the Alamo went on. He heard the screams of the wounded, the whistling and crump of shells as the battered walls gave way. He smelled the stench and smoke and felt again the weakness in him, brought about by days of no sleep and little food and water.

He saw the encouraging face of his sergeant father, bloodied and his eyes so sad for his son.

'Courage, boy, you'll make it. Forget your duty .Forget that trumpet. Get you down into the sewer and hide there, and go now!' It was an order from a sergeant to one of his men. Again the words rang in Ben's ears and now, as he strove to climb the rock face to get to his enemy, he was at last losing that guilt he'd always endured for being alive when all the rest had been massacred. . . .

The sneering arrogant Mexican face came to him again, as it had been thirty years ago. Coronel Fernandez who'd carried out General Santa Anna's orders with such devilish gusto. The bastard had enjoyed the utter annihilation of the one hundred and eighty surviving Texicans of the siege on that black day, 6 March, 1836.

He didn't fear for himself any more. All he wanted was to kill the smiling sneering bastard. That was what his life had been for. To toughen himself and make him an expert climber. God had planned it that way. He was the one destined to send that fiend to hell. . . .

Ben lay gasping at the top of the rock face. His respite was soon over. He dragged himself upright and surveyed the whole panorama of the gorge. It was a wonderful sight, the sun beginning to go down, the long shaft of the gorge even now moving into shadow. He took deep breaths to ease his pounding heart. He saw the small group with heads uplifted watching him far below. He waved. They waved back. Then he turned and trotted away.

He saw the tiny dot of a figure stumbling towards the far peak. The way was rough and the wind cutting, but Ben only felt the acrid sweat dripping down into his eyes, stinging them. He paused to wipe away the drops on the bloodied kerchief about his hand.

He was too far away to use his Colt on the fleeing man. He didn't want that. His gun would only be used if all else failed. He wanted to look into the man's eyes as he died. He wanted him to know that a witness still lived who'd seen and heard things a sixteen-year-old boy should never experience before he'd hidden like some sewer-rat, a shivering vomiting child crying for his dead mother. . . .

The steep incline leading to the great peak that Ben had known all his life but never explored, was now covered with a powdering of snow. The wind was keen at this height and breathing more difficult. As he pushed his way upwards, the snow became deeper and harder and soon he was labouring and moving slowly.

Grimly he kept on. If that bastard who must be at least ten or fifteen years older than himself could do it, so could he.

He saw with satisfaction that El Condor moved stiffly, head hanging low. The dog's turd was already suffering. He also looked as if he was limping. Good. May every muscle and bone in him crack and give him the torments of hell!

Ben was surprised when El Condor summoned up enough strength to tackle the peak. It reared high in the sky as if straining up and away from the rest of the ridge of mountains. The waning sun highlighted the frosted snow, blinding in its intensity. Now Ben knew that he was chasing a madman. This climb was to be the end of both of them. The climb would lead to nowhere, to oblivion.

Ben's mouth stretched back in a joyous abandon, showing white teeth amidst a mass of black bristles. Well, he'd always known their lives would be interwoven. He'd become a man of the mountains. Now he would die on this peak.

He knew his mind was beginning to wander. Lack of oxygen, no doubt. The long-ago nightmares were part of it. But beneath the euphoria of hunting El Condor was the small thin thread of reason that he still controlled. He might be mad, as El Condor was, but he still had his reason. He must move with caution. After all these agonizing hours of pursuing the man, he had to have the privilege of seeing him die. He must not fail.

Darkness came swiftly and with it such a cold as Ben had never experienced before. It thickened his blood, making him clumsy. He wondered how El Condor was faring, for neither, of them wore clothes sufficient to keep out the cold. Ben wondered if he would be cheated by nature herself. Would the bastard live through the night, or would he find a frozen body?

He found an aperture in the rock and crouched down out of the wind. It would serve while he ate the last of his food and drank the last of his water, then threw away the canteen. He wouldn't need that any more.

He considered his chances. The going was not as steep as the rock face in the gorge. The way led upwards in gentle terraces, and there were signs that wild goats climbed faint trails in the middle of summer. The sweat on him turned to ice and he knew he had to move on. He couldn't lie up for the night, for to sleep would mean death.

Fortunately a three-quarter moon was showing, and the stars with it seemed low and bright. He could move on if he took his time and put one foot in front of the other in case of hidden crevices.

He wondered if El Condor was still moving ahead.

The dark moonlit hours seemed to go on for ever. Ben's brain was numb with only one thought, move on, damn you! He can do it, so can you!

Then the first streaks of a rosy-golden glow rose from behind the ridge of mountains and cast an illusion of warmth across the glistening snow. He looked upwards and saw the faint trail left behind by El Condor. He too had forced his body onwards. Ben saw too that the trail was wavering as if El Condor was losing his strength fast.

Ben was thinking like an animal now, his teeth showed in a wolfish snarl, his prey was nearer than he'd expected.

His eyes, encrusted with frost were bleary now. He knew that his body was already closing down. He cursed himself for his human weakness and whipped that fire of anger in his belly to give him that extra strength. If he died before he could extract his vengeance on that devilish *coronel*, his soul would remain in limbo for ever, seeking and not finding.

He shook his head to free him from such thoughts. He would not fail.

Then he began the long last climb, and as the sun rose and blossomed, changing the cold hell of night into a glorious, wondrous dawn, he saw his quarry in front of him, not a hundred yards ahead. The hunched figure was sitting on a jutting snow-covered rock, his head in his hands.

For a wild moment, Ben thought he was frozen in death; then the haggard face slowly lifted and they stared at each other.

Then, drunkenly, as if it was too heavy to lift, Ben heaved his trumpet aloft, the sun's rays touching it, sending forth a blinding golden light. Then mockingly he put the mouthpiece to his lips and attempted to play the last post. The notes came squeakily for Ben's breath was gasping and also the trumpet was frozen up. But El Condor's head came up sharply. He knew and understood.

Wearily he stood up and stretched frozen limbs. He shouted to Ben, his voice sounding eerie in the thin morning air.

'If you want me, come and get me!' He began a stumbling run that ended when he fell to his knees. Then began the agonizing crawl.

Ben's weakening heart leapt exultantly. The bastard was down. It was only a matter of forcing his tired body upwards for another hundred yards, but those yards seemed twice as far. Why didn't the son of a bitch stop and let him catch up? Didn't the swine know that he, Ben, had to get rid of all that fire and corroding anger within him?

He saw El Condor crawl to a ridge underneath an overhang and watched him drag himself upright and lean against the sheltered wall, and Ben gritted his teeth. He knew El Condor had chosen the place for the confrontation.

El Condor was calmly contemplating the awe-inspiring vista of far mountain peaks and the valleys below when finally Ben reached the ridge. He did not attempt to attack Ben as he could have done. Each man knew there was no future for either of them. Only madmen would climb mountains with no way of escape. This was as far as they could get towards heaven while still on earth.

Gasping, Ben drew himself up and faced El Condor. He saw not the man of his nightmares any longer. This was a burnt-out old man, not even El Condor any more. Just a weary old man. And what was he? Just another weary tired-out man of forty-six going on sixty. Life was over for both of them. He swayed but his weakness was only physical. The loathing for what the women and children went through before the siege ended, the wounded lying in makeshift cots and murdered as they lay helpless, the torturing of those still on their feet, remained in his mind. They had to be avenged as well as his father who'd died along with the rest.

But what stood out in Ben's mind was the much younger Coronel Fernandez, laughing and using his sword like a butcher dismembering a carcass as he ran along the aisle between the beds in the makeshift hospital. That had been Ben Jackson's last sight of the *coronel* before Ben had run and dropped into the stinking sewer.

'So, Coronel Fernandez, do you remember the young trumpeter who encouraged the garrison at the Alamo?'

El Condor's eyes half closed against the glare of the sun.

'I don't remember you but I remember the defiance you whipped up with your playing. Even my men commented on it. So you're the one who's haunted me all these years?'

'The one and the same, Coronel. I wanted you to

141

know that I should get you some day.'

'So you think you've got me, eh?'

'It looks like it. But it's not the same, is it? You're not the the man you once were. You're not even a hawk, never mind a condor.' He sounded disappointed, as if robbed of something.

El Condor laughed.

'What were you expecting? A man still in his passionate youth? You're not a wet-behind-the-ears cadet any more with a penchant for rallying the troops! So, what do we do about it?'

They glared at each other, instinctively crouching and waiting, both oblivious of wind and numbing cold. They watched each other's eyes and Ben was nearly fooled by the sudden flick of El Condor's half-hidden arm. He was just in time to see the wicked glint of the knife as it came handle over blade towards his heart.

He lunged sideways and forward as it shot over the edge and into the air to bounce and leap downwards, lost for ever.

Then his numbed hands closed about El Condor and they heaved and wrestled on the edge away from the overhang and at the mercy of the wind.

Ben clawed at the man's eyes while El Condor attempted a bear-hug.

'If I go, you go,' panted El Condor, his eyes gleaming with madness as he strove for a firmer hold.

Ben's knee came up and caught him in the crotch. His face contorted and his hold loosened, giving Ben the opportunity to kick out again. This time he missed, but as El Condor leapt back he felt the ground give beneath him and he twisted in the air with arms flung out as he plummeted downwards, bouncing, his body limp as it hit both snow and boulders.

Ben drew back, breathing hard. He rubbed his frozen cheeks, all at once weak and helpless. It was over, the long years of waiting, finished for ever.

He laughed, head up, facing the sky, in a mad kind of euphoria. He felt as if he had all the power in the world coursing through him.

'Thank you God for allowing me this moment in time!'

Then, as if that prayer was a signal, the wind dropped and Ben was conscious of a vibration he hadn't been aware of before. It sounded like . . . He looked upwards and the rush of victory was drained from him. Now he knew the presentiment he'd had earlier was coming true. There was no way off this mountain for him. He had climbed to nowhere.

He stood waiting, calm in his knowledge. The end would come fast; he didn't care any more. He'd done what he had to do.

The vibration turned into the noise of thunder and then the avalanche from the top of the peak rolled down and enveloped him on its grinding ruthless way to the bottom.

A lonely condor wheeled high into the air and away from the danger of avalanche, his great flapping wings leisurely sweeping the sky, his eyes piercing the thin air, looking for any creature that moved.

He saw a tiny bird winging its way to its nest and changed course. No carrion today off the mountain. He would have to settle for a smaller victim.

He swooped and pounced, his claws satisfyingly firmly embedded in the flesh of the bird. He flew away and the mountain peak was once again a desolate lonely place.

Far below in the gorge the morning sun crept over the sleeping camp. Jeff Onslow woke with a start, his gaze on Lucia da Silva who was sleeping wrapped in a blanket not far from Tijuana. Ely and Red lay a little away from the others. Automatically he looked for Wang and then remembered Wang was no more. He would miss the little man.

He got up and kicked the smouldering embers of the fire to a blaze and piled on some wood left over from last night. Soon he had the coffee-pot bubbling and the smell of coffee woke the others.

It was still early, the sun not far above the distant skyline. They crowded about the fire, rubbing chilled hands as Lucia poured coffee for them all.

Jeff doled out what was left of their bread and cold meat.

'We've got to get out of here fast. This is the last of the grub,' he announced. All knew what it would mean to be caught in these desolate mountains without food or water.

'What about Ben?' Tijuana asked as his strong teeth tore into a chunk of dried meat.

'What about him?' Jeff asked tersely.

'Well . . .' Tijuana's voice tailed off as he looked from Jeff to Ely. 'You don't think he'll come back?'

'For the love of God, man, use your head! Only madmen would climb that rock face and then carry on up the mountain. El Condor knew it and so did Ben, but he was loco from the start. God knows what happened up there and there was the night to get through. No, Ben will not come back. We can pack up and go as soon as we're ready.'

Tijuana grinned.

'So, it's all over? The camp's gone and El Condor will never fly again.'

'A nice way of putting it.We'll go back to San Antonio and let the good townsfolk know they have nothing to fear any longer. Maybe they'll still want me for sheriff,' Jeff said hopefully.

Ely grinned.

'Knowing you, you won't last very long. I can't see you settling down as sheriff of a backwater town. What about ridin' along with me?'

'Well, there was a woman . . .'

'Hell, Jeff, there's women everywhere. Who wants to be tied down?' He looked at Lucia da Silva apologetically. 'Beg pardon, ma'am, no disrespect intended.'

Lucia smiled faintly.

'I understand, and none taken.'

'I want you to know ma'am,' Ely went on, 'that we think you're real ace, ma'am, not complainin' none and helpin' us with the hosses and such.'

She smiled again, this time wearily.

'I'm glad it's over and I can be on my way.'

'What will you do, ma'am?'

'Go on to Montelova.' She looked at Tijuana.'I'm hoping . . .' she stopped and Tijuana put a hand out and covered hers.

'I'm going to Montelova with her and then, who knows?'

Jeff nodded and grinned. He'd half thought of making a play for her himself, but the memory of Miranda Parker's luscious body had stopped him. Besides, Lucia's strong-mindedness had partially put him off. He liked a woman to be compliant. He wondered if Miranda was still in San Antonio or had she moved on?

If she was still there, Ely was going to be disappointed. He would either have to settle down himself or move on alone. . . .

There was only one way to find out.

'That's it folks! Time to ride!'

Soon they'd packed up, dowsed the fire, saddled up and were ready to move out.

It was a pity about Wang, Jeff thought as he cinched up his saddle. He'd miss the little devil. It was a pity he couldn't leave a marker for him, but Wang would understand, being a heathen and all that. He wouldn't appreciate a cross. Maybe it was all for the best, seeing he'd lost his son who'd been all the world to him. He'd not been the same old Wang since the boy's death.

Then his thoughts turned to Miranda Parker. He thought of her lush body and hoped she was still in town. He could do with a bit of womanly pampering after all this. . . .

Red put a hand on his arm.

'You hear what I hear, boss?'

Then Jeff became aware of a faint growling in the air and the ground beneath them vibrated. He looked up sharply. It wasn't thunder. The whole party were staring towards the far peaks. Then he saw it. The glistening of the early morning sun's rays on moving snow. An avalanche!

They watched, awed, as the slow-moving mass, gathering momentum, tumbled down the mountain from the peak.

They stood in silence thinking of the two men out there somewhere. Lucia covered her eyes and her lips moved silently in prayer. Red took off his hat and wiped his forehead, then spat. Then he spoke.

'There's one thing for sure. If anyone hears a trumpet playin' again, it sure will be a ghost that plays it!'

In the early morning sky, a lone condor wheeled and circled, already seeking out new prey. Jeff turned to the others.

'All right, everyone, let's move out!'

Nine

It was fiesta time in San Antonio from the moment old Pegleg, sitting on his veranda, spied the weary bunch riding into town. He'd called to Mama Geraldi's son Juan to run and tell the mayor and anyone else drinking at Eduardo Antonini's makeshift bar in the town square.

Then, as Jeff flanked by Ely and Red along with the woman, with the town's volunteers behind, spread out and trotted down the street, a great cry went up and a great crowd gathered and watched silently as they approached; even the whores hanging over their upper walkway, remained silent. Waiting.

Jeff glanced sideways at a tired, dirty Lucia, looking gaunt with hard riding and then at the rest of the sorry bunch. He and all of them were in bad shape. It was good to be back.

The mayor stepped forward and looked up at Jeff. 'Well, *señor?*'

Jeff nodded slowly and wearily. His neck was all seized up.

'It's over. El Condor and his men are kaput!'

The words were a signal for cheering; several women forced themselves through the crowd and threw themselves at the volunteers, hugging and kissing them as the news was conveyed from mouth to mouth.

Men caught their womenfolk and jigged them up and down as the laughter and cheering swelled to a roar. The whores hanging over their veranda-rails hollered, swishing their skirts and showing their bloomers in delight and Red, taking one look, slipped from his horse, tossed his reins to Ely and, winking, made for the outer staircase. For the girls, it meant no more hellish nights to be endured with outlaws who wouldn't pay for what they got.

Eduardo rushed over with a flagon of rotgut whiskey and held it high while they all took a long pull. Even Lucia drank and choked on it, but it put new life into her. All she wanted was a bath to ease her sore backside and legs and a feather bed to lie on and sleep for ever.

Within hours, the Mexican flag flew over what was the sheriff's office and jail, smaller flags were draped from verandas, musicians appeared mysteriously and guitars played along with drums, a squeaky violin and a battered old squeeze-box. They made up a good orchestra and soon they were playing the traditional Mexican tunes, which were the signal for couples to begin dancing.

Eduardo grinned and ordered his wife and her

149

helpers to broach more barrels. If the town's stores were closed for the day, his bar would be open and he would make a good profit. His eyes gleamed. Soon, he would be able to rebuild his saloon and it would be better than the old one could ever have been.

The mayor ushered the newcomers into his own home despite townsfolk wanting to shake hands and pat backs. There, Lucia was allowed to bathe first and, after borrowing clean clothes from the mayor's rather buxom wife, she ate. Jeff, Ely and Tijuana took a hasty bath in near-cold water and in borrowed shirts, joined Lucia.

The mayor listened avidly to Jeff's report and nodded his head at intervals.

'You have done well, *señors.*' He nodded at all of them. 'And the *señora* showed great bravery. You are all heroes and will share in the reward that the town comittee have decided upon with the approval of the people themselves!'

Ely and Tijuana sat up, now alert at the mention of reward. Jeff was more relaxed. The mayor had hinted at a reward if Jeff was successful before they'd left San Antonio.

'Er . . . how how much would that be?' Ely asked, thinking that it would be a good boost when he left San Antonio for good.

The mayor looked a bit apologetic. He coughed.

'Well, it's not as much as we should like, *señors.* We are but a poor people here in San Antonio, but we have gathered together a hundred dol . . .' he stopped at Ely's disgusted look and went on hurriedly, 'a hundred and fifty dollars.' He smiled and looked at them all. Looking at Lucia, he said apologetically, 'We did not count on a lady . . . no offence, *señora.*'

Lucia shrugged her shoulders.

'*Señor*, I do not expect any reward. My life and freedom from that . . . that . . . devil, is all the reward I ask.' Then she looked at Tijuana and said softly, 'I've already had my reward.' She smiled at him.

The mayor sighed. Oh, what it was to be young and resilient and in love! Then he got back to practicalities.

'You, Sheriff, I take it you will be staying with us?'

Jeff moved uneasily, aware of Ely's meaningful gaze. He knew well the old boy wanted him to move on. San Antonio would be a sleepy place to spend the rest of one's life.

'I'm not sure yet. It depends . . .' he began. The mayor looked uncertain.

'The townsfolk expect . . . we have a house for you . . . not in very good repair but it could be made good. We're willing . . .' He stopped and looked at Jeff's set face. He lifted his arms in silent plea. 'Please think about it. We should be happier with a tough sheriff walking our streets.'

'I said it would depend.'

'Then please tell me soon what your decision is.'

Outside the mayor's house the sounds of revelry

were rising as Eduardo's beer-barrels emptied. Tijuana took Lucia to join in the fun and Ely settled for a pipe on the mayor's veranda, for his old bones still creaked.

Jeff, impatient to find Miranda, disappeared into the crowd and it was some time before he found her dancing with a tall bearded Americano, an obvious stranger to San Antonio. He looked like a gambler in Jeff's eyes, black suit, white frilled shirt and string tie, with a black hat with silver conches around the crown and a serviceable Colt holstered at his waist. Not a man to confront, or one that would allow the woman he was dancing with to be taken from him.

Jeff leaned against a wooden upright and waited, his blood aflame at the sight of the buxom flesh, showing rounded milky-white shoulders and the hint of black-stockinged legs as her skirts swirled high in the air. He had an itch he couldn't scratch.

Why hadn't she come to him as soon as she knew he was back in town? A little voice spoke in the back of his head. 'Don't be a fool. She's interested in that big bloated slug.'

He turned away and took advantage of Eduardo's invitation to drink on the house seeing he was the local hero.

He was staggering a little and glassy-eyed when at last he saw Miranda standing by herself, waiting for her gambler to go and relieve himself in some back alley.

'Miranda, I must talk to you!' He pulled her away

152

from the alley where she was waiting for the big man. He startled her.

'Jeff! I was meaning to speak to you but you were with a woman . . .' she began, then stopped at the glow in Jeff's eyes.

He pulled her into the shadow of a shade-tree and kissed her, his arms holding her close. He smelled the hot sweetness of her and he wanted to eat her. Christ! How he wanted her!

'Let's go up to your room,' he whispered into her soft bosom. She tried to push him away, striking his chest and his arms clamped about her like a vice.

'Jeff! You're hurting me! I can't breathe!' His hold loosened. He shook her as gently as his passion would let him.

'Miranda, what's the matter with you? I thought you and I had something special between us.'

Her bosom rose and fell in agitation, her face taking on a hard cold frozen look.

'Jeff, you can't come back and expect me to be waiting and ready to fall into bed, the minute you want me! I've other plans, Jeff. I'm leaving San Antonio.'

'Well, that's all right with me. I'll come with you.'

'You don't understand.'

'It's *you* who don't understand, Miranda. I want to marry you. I don't want you just as a friendly whore. I want you as my wife. We could stay here. They've offered me a house. You'd be somebody, the wife of the sheriff. Doesn't that mean something?'

She laughed, and the cynical sound made his spine crawl.

'Me respectable in San Antonio? You must be mad! I'll never be respectable in San Antonio! You know that or you're a fool!'

He stared at her. This wasn't the soft passionate creature of his imaginings. This was a stranger, the real Miranda Parker. She was right. He was a fool.

'I've said we can go wherever you wish,' he began uncertainly, not knowing if he really wanted that. She laughed again, this time with cutting mockery.

'You think marriage is all a girl like me wants? That I should be grateful that you've marriage in mind? Well, let me tell you something, Jeff Onslow, if I wanted marriage, I should choose someone with far better prospects than such as you!' Her look of contempt swept him from scuffed boots to the top of his dusty Stetson.

Then the big bloated man was by her side, looking sharply at at him, then at her.

'This man troublin' you, sweetheart?'

She smiled up at him and tucked her hand through his arm.

'No, Josh, just tying up loose ends. Come on, we've wasted enough time. How are you on the polka?' She swept him away with a whirl of skirts leaving behind a faint musky scent.

Damn all women! Jeff went in search of Ely. They would pick up their reward money and leave San Antonio tomorrow!

Ely was still on the veranda, a half-empty jug of rotgut whiskey at his feet, his pipe out and held loosely in relaxed fingers. He was snoring heavily.

Jeff poked him hard and he awakened with a curse, his right hand going for his gun.

'What in hell's name . . .' he began, then stopped at the look on Jeff's face. 'She didn't want to know eh?' he finished and reached for the jug. 'Here, have a drink. No woman's worth gettin' yer bowels in an uproar.' He took a swig himself before handing it over.

Jeff shook his head.

'I've had enough. We'll be on our way in the morning, first light. Nothing to stay here for.'

Ely grunted.

'Well, I couldn't see you settlin' in this one-eyed hole. Now that El Condor's off the scene, it'll go back to sleep. We need excitement, you and me. We'd die otherwise.' He laughed and belched. 'Maybe we should call it a day and hit the sack if we're gonna have an early start.'

Jeff helped the older man up out of the rocking-chair. Ely groaned a little, cursing his stiffened knees.

'That does it! I'm not meant to loaf around. I gotta keep movin'.'

Jeff laughed. 'You old son of a gun, that's only an excuse to keep drifting. But I'll go along with it.' Then he stopped and lifted his head. 'God dammit, is that shooting I hear?'

Both listened. The shooting was intermingled now

with screams and the music in the background had ceased.

'What in hell's happening out there?' He began to run down the street towards the square, Ely, despite his stiffness, following at a goodly pace.

A distraught mayor met them as they neared the crowd of revellers, now scrambling away from the square. He clutched Jeff by the shirtfront.

'Thank God you're here, Sheriff! We've got trouble in there.' The mayor nodded in the direction of the square itself. 'Buckwheat Pete has just rode into town with his gang of cut-throats and is shootin' up the town. He's taken some of the women hostage! Do something, Sheriff!'

'But . . .' Jeff stopped himself. He was about to say that he wasn't sheriff any more, but Ely's eyes were glinting with the excitement of battle. He sighed and then laughed. What the hell . . . The town needed them both. He looked at the mayor.

'Right. Let's get at 'em. How many men can we rely on?'

The mayor's anxious face broke into a smile.

'That means you're staying? There's half a dozen guns waiting in the alley. All they want is a leader.'

'Then they've got one, maybe two,' Jeff glanced at Ely. 'What about it, Ely? Will you be my deputy?'

Ely grinned, stretched out a hand and touched Jeff's palm.

'If this li'l old town throws up a mess of outlaws every once in a while, I'm yer man, Sheriff Onslow.

156

So let's get in there and cause a bit of mayhem. Right?'

The mayor grinned, relieved that at last someone was going to take permanent charge of the town. He could relax and put his feet up and maybe live long enough to become a grandpa. . . .

As Jeff looked over the small bunch of volunteer deputies and gave orders on rounding up the drunken outlaws and rescuing the women, Ely reflected that maybe it was a good thing settling down in one place. After all, his knees wouldn't last for ever.

R